Bolshevik Salute

A Modernist Chinese Novel

Bolshevik Salute

A Modernist
Chinese Novel

WANG MENG

*Translated,
with Introduction and critical essay,
by WENDY LARSON*

UNIVERSITY OF WASHINGTON PRESS

Seattle and London

6 [9o ฿ แт   1 ๅ. 9 6

Library of Congress Cataloging-in-Publication Data
Wang, Meng.
    Bolshevik salute : a modernist Chinese novel / Wang Meng ;
    translated, with introduction and critical essay by Wendy Larson.
          p.   cm.
    ISBN 0-295-96856-7 (alk. paper) :
    I. Larson, Wendy.   II. Title.
PL2919.M39B65   1989
895.1'352—dc20   89-22525
                                                           CIP

To my father,
Morris Larson

Contents

Foreword to the English Edition

WANG MENG

The people's revolution was inspired by sacred beliefs. Because the revolution was great and victorious, the people were uplifted, and worshiped it. But those who threw their lives into revolution—especially the young—received nothing but inexplicable persecution and retaliation, carried out against them in the name of revolution. Was this an absurd tragedy? Was this an experiment that could not be avoided? Was this a universal law of history? Was this worthwhile, or was it a total waste?

But no matter how we evaluate history, how we evaluate each character in history, we cannot blot out the experiences that are engraved on our bones and written in our hearts. Perhaps this kind of experience will never be understood or gain sympathy, but at the very least it should inspire some reflection or a brief sigh.

I extend my thanks to Wendy Larson for translating into English my novel *Bolshevik Salute*, a work which expresses the personal experiences and processes of my innermost being, and for allowing American readers, who live in an entirely different environment, to experience to some small degree this unique struggle.

Acknowledgments

I want to thank the Committee for Scholarly Communication with the People's Republic of China for giving me two years of support to study and do research at Beijing University from 1979 to 1981, when, among other things, I first met Wang Meng and drafted a translation of *Bolshevik Salute*. I want to thank Wang Meng, not only for contributing so richly to contemporary Chinese literature but also for encouraging me in this translation. Also, I would like to thank Ted Huters, who gave me valuable suggestions on the translation and essay and a great deal of fruitful advice on my study of Chinese modernism; Kyna Rubin, who checked over parts of the translation when I was first working on it and corrected many errors; Phil Williams, who read the essay and pointed out many inconsistencies; and Yue Daiyun, who enlightened me with her discussions of Wang Meng's work and her fine teaching of modern and contemporary Chinese literature. Special thanks go to my husband, Xu Luo, who responded gracefully to my endless questions about contemporary politics, language use, and customs, and enriched my understanding of the last thirty years of Chinese history with examples from his own experience.

My translation is based on the original publication of *Bolshevik Salute* which appeared in the literary journal *Dangdai*, March 1979.

Wendy Larson
University of Oregon

Introduction

Wang Meng and the Modernist
Controversy in Contemporary China

For those unfamiliar with the literary history of the People's
Republic of China, the publication of modernist works after
the death of Mao Zedong in 1976 may not seem to be a great
event. To scholars and others following the political and literary movements of China, however, the relatively wide-
spread emergence of modernism marks a radical break with
the past. The Chinese literary works that were produced in
the late 1970s and first half of the 1980s broke precedent
with the socialist realism of the post-1949 era and even with
the critical realism of the May Fourth decade of the 1920s.
In the decade following the Cultural Revolution, which offi-
cially ended with the death of Mao Zedong and the arrest of
the Gang of Four in 1976, Chinese writers began to experiment with a form of literary expression that, with very few
exceptions, had not existed on the Chinese mainland since
the poetic experiments of Dai Wangshu and Li Jinfa in the
1930s. After these early attempts at modernist poetry,
which included the pioneering efforts of the "New Sensibil-
ity Group" (*Xin ganjue pai*) in the thirties, the political situation in China favored a more socially engaged literature
that would actively work to resist the Japanese aggression
of the thirties and forties. At least in the Yan'an area, where
Communist authorities were forging the literary ideology
that would become the foundation of literary politics on the
mainland after 1949, modernism and other forms of literature that did not carry an overt political or social message
were not as popular as works that promoted class struggle,

land reform, or other kinds of social progress. Meanwhile, a modernist movement developed on Taiwan in the 1960s, and has continued to flourish, resulting in the production of contemporary masterpieces such as *Man with His Back to the Sea (Beihai de ren)* by Wang Wenxing.

In the late 1970s and early 1980s, mainland writers began to utilize modernist styles again, writing drama, fiction, and poetry in ways that shocked readers accustomed to more straightforward techniques. Modernist poetry was dubbed "obscure" (*menglong*) by baffled critics and political authorities, who criticized modernist writers for disregarding the definition of literature that had been standard ideology (if not always standard practice) since the late 1930s—a definition which stipulated that literary writing was a socially engaged, mass-oriented art form. Modernism, critics claimed, was aimed not at the general population, but at a highly educated minority that would not be put off by narrative discontinuity, ungrammatical sentences, breaks in chronology, and excessive psychological probing. Furthermore, modernist writers were criticized as imitators of the West who could serve their country better by taking both their material and their form from native soil. Critics pointed out that not only was modernism Western in origin, but—since it developed rapidly in the same period as imperialism and capitalistic expansion—it was also politically suspect. Even worse, they claimed, modernism destroyed the principle of writing as a reflection of social problems that had been established through the use of socialist and critical realism, replacing it with a detached, difficult style that probed the psychological deficiencies of a politically unaware minority. Modernist writers, according to the critics, used literature not to improve society, but to cast doubt on the theoretical and practical foundations of socialist society.[1]

The emergence of modernism in post-Mao China is a complex phenomenon with many causes. Attempting to defend their writing from critics who have focused on the political and social unsuitability of modernism to Chinese society, some modernist writers have singled out the devastating effect of the ten years of the Cultural Revolution on all aspects of Chinese life, particularly in the psychological perception of identity and culture, as a major reason for the development of modernism. According to these writers, ideas that

1. There have been hundreds of articles and books published in China on modernism. Some of the most detailed or controversial are Gao Xingjian, *Initial Investigations into the Technique of Modern Fiction (Xiandai xiaoshuo jiqiao chutan)* (Guangdong: Huacheng chubanshe, 1981); Xu Chi, "Modernization and Modernism" *(Xiandaihua yu xiandaipai)*, *Waiguo wenxue yanjiu*, 1982, no. 1:115–17; Xu Jingya, "A Flourishing Group of Poets" *(Jueqi de shiqun)*, *Dangdai wenxue sichao*, 1983, no. 1:14–27. English readers can find translations of some documents and discussion of the issues in *Trees on the Mountain: An Anthology of New Chinese Writing*, ed. Stephen C. Soong and John Minford, (Hong Kong: Renditions, Chinese University Press, 1984). See also William Tay, "'Obscure Poetry': A Controversy in Post-Mao China," in *After Mao: Chinese Literature and Society, 1978–1981*, Jeffrey C. Kinkley, ed. (Cambridge, Mass.: The Council on East Asian Studies, Harvard University, 1985), 133–58; William Tay, "Wang Meng, Stream of Consciousness, and the Controversy over Modernism," *Modern Chinese Literature*, 1, no. 1 (1984): 7–24; D. E. Pollard, "The Controversy Over Modernism, 1979–84," *The China Quarterly*, no. 104 (December 1985): 641–56; Bonnie McDougall, "Bei Dao's Poetry: Revelation and Communication," *Modern Chinese Literature*, 1, no. 2 (1985):225–52; Wendy Larson, "Realism, Modernism, and the Anti–'Spiritual Pollution' Campaign," *Modern China*, 15, no. 1 (1989): 37–71.

previously were accepted by the majority of people came
under severe scrutiny as the political edifice crumbled and
was replaced by a semi-capitalist economy embracing an
ideology scorned a few years before. Modernist writers and
pro-modernist critics pointed to the destruction of ideologi-
cal unity, psychological fluctuation, and loss of faith in socialist goals as valid conditions for the emergence of *native*
modernist traditions.

In 1980 a campaign against "bourgeois liberalism" was
getting under way, and the work of Wang Meng, the present
Minister of Culture but at that time a professional writer,
was involved in a series of discussions on literary modernism and its political implications. These discussions occurred
three years before the major Anti–"Spiritual Pollution"
Campaign of 1983, which took the books of some modernists
off the shelves of bookstores. One of Wang Meng's modernist novellas, *Bolshevik Salute (Buli)*, which was published in
1979, became a focal point of the debate. *Bolshevik Salute*
revolves around the life of an intellectual Party member
named Zhong Yicheng from the 1950s through the 1970s,
with flashbacks to some of his work for the Party when he
was a teenager in the late forties. The book has little action
and almost no plot; much of the writing consists of the psychological meanderings of the protagonist as he tries to
understand his situation. The similarity between the fate of
Zhong Yicheng and that of Wang Meng has led some critics
to call the novella autobiographical; at the same time, the
political difficulty of reconciling Wang's high status as a pa-
triotic if innovative writer with the criticism of literary modernism as a decadent Western import has led others to represent his work as realism, or as a type of distinctly Chinese

modernism that uses modernist techniques but maintains a focus on social and political affairs more characteristic of realism.[2]

Like the protagonist Zhong Yicheng, Wang Meng (1934–), a Communist Party worker from Hebei, became a Party member very young, before his fourteenth birthday in 1948. In 1949 he was transferred to Beijing, where he worked as a Party secretary in the Communist Youth League. In August of that year he entered a Party school to study political theory. In 1953, when he was nineteen, Wang published his first novel, *Springtime Forever (Qingchun wansui)*. His publication of "A Young Man Arrives at the Organization Department" *(Zuzhibu laile ge nianging ren)* in 1956 led to a serious attack in the 1957 Anti-Rightist Campaign and his subsequent exile from Beijing to the countryside, where he worked in manual labor for five years. Foreshadowing some of the themes of *Bolshevik Salute*, "A Young Man" depicts a young and naive bureaucrat who cannot accept the waste, corruption, and sterility of Party bureaucracy and attempts to make reforms. The story was interpreted as an overly critical attack on the Communist Party. In 1962, Wang was transferred·back to Beijing and taught in the Chinese Department of Beijing Normal College, but in 1963 he was again transferred—in effect exiled—to the Xinjiang Province branch of the Chinese Writers' Association. In 1965, at the inception of the Cultural Revolution, Wang was sent to a commune in Xinjiang to participate in manual labor. In 1973 he was transferred to the Xinjiang Ministry of Culture,

2. See Li Tuo, "Realism and Stream-of-Consciousness" (*Xianshizhuyi he yishiliu*), *Shiyue*, April 1980: 239–44.

where he continued studying Uighur—the language of the
minority population of the province—translated stories
from Uighur into Chinese, and started work on a novel
about life in the Xinjiang countryside. Wang came back to
Beijing in 1979, after the fall of the Gang of Four, and
worked as a professional writer in the Chinese Writers' Association. He began to publish stories and novellas, and in
1980 his modernist works "Eye of the Night" *(Ye de yan)*,
"Sound of Spring" *(Chun zhi sheng)*, "Fluttering Tail of the
Kite" *(Fengzheng piaodai)*, "Dream of the Sea" *(Hai de
meng)*, and "Butterfly" *(Hudie)*, as well as *Bolshevik Salute*
were criticized as anti-realist, non-Marxist, and un-Chinese
by a battery of anti-modernist critics. In 1986, Wang Meng
was appointed Minister of Culture.[3]

Wang Meng has defended his modernist work as spring-
ing from his own experience in the last "thirty years" and
through the "eight thousand *li*" he has traveled, and as influenced not only by Western modernism, but by Chinese literary traditions and contemporary art forms as well:

> I have experimented with psychological description that
> can break through temporal limitations and fully illus-
> trate the "eight thousand *li*" and "thirty years" I have
> spoken of, and the various relationships and contrasts be-
> tween the things and experiences of these eight thousand
> *li* and thirty years. I sought out the past, the present,
> foreign and Chinese works, and the goal of my seeking is

3. Critical articles about Wang Meng's work and its position in
the controversy about modernism are collected in *Materials on the
Fiction and Recent Work of Wang Meng (Wang Meng xiaoshuo
chuangxin ziliao)* (Beijing: Renmin daxue chubanshe, 1980).

the "self" of creation. I do not deny that I have learned
from other works, not only foreign works but also the poetry of Li Shangyin and Li He, and the comedy crosstalk
of Hou Baolin and Ma Ji. But the form of my experiment
comes from the soil under my own feet, from our own
lives. Only with the new complexity and rapid rhythm of
our lives can our fiction become multi-faceted and fast-
rhythmed.[4]

Although the experiences of Zhong Yicheng in *Bolshevik
Salute* may not correspond exactly to those of the author, it
is clear that much of the story comes directly from his own
experiences during the golden years of the 1950s when the
authority of Mao Zedong and the Communist Party was
strongest, the crisis of the Anti-Rightist Movement of 1957
when hundreds of intellectuals were criticized and sent to
do manual labor, and the physically and mentally painful
Cultural Revolution years of the 1960s and 1970s. As the
story ends, the reader is conscious that a new political and
social era is beginning. As a well-crafted tale that some Chinese readers read as a revolutionary modernist experiment
and others as a continuation of a vital Chinese realism that
had been temporarily displaced, *Bolshevik Salute* also marks
the beginning of a new era for writers in China. The debates

4. Li Shangyin (813–858) and Li He (1527–1602) are poets whose
works are considered relatively difficult and obscure. Hou Baolin
and Ma Ji are contemporary comedians who specialize in comedy
cross-talk, which is similar to stand-up comedy but done with two
people, one usually playing the foil. Wang Meng, "What Am I Seek-
ing?" (*Wo zai xunzhao shemma?*), ibid., p. 105; originally published
in *Wenyi bao*, October 1980:42–44.

that have surrounded it clearly designate the contemporary
period of Chinese literature as one of controversy and interest, an era that is generating the most thought-provoking
literary questions of the last thirty years.

W. L.

Bolshevik
Salute

**A Modernist
Chinese Novel**

I

Strangely hot weather. The forecast in P—— said the temperature would go up to 39°C today. This is the temperature at which your fever sends you to the emergency room, your head hurts, you're dizzy, your lips crack, you can't eat, yellow fuzz grows on your tongue; it's the temperature that turns your face pale and your lips brown, and though you cover yourself with two layers of quilts, you can't get warm. You touch the table, the wall, the bedpost—they're all warm. You touch the stone and metal utensils—they burn your hand. You touch your body, but it's as cold as ice. Zhong Yicheng's heart was colder still.

But what's going on here? Suddenly, in a split second, everything freezes. The flowers, the sky, the air, the newspapers, the sound of laughter, and people's faces instantly harden. Has the temperature abruptly fallen to that of outer space—absolute zero? The sky looks like pale slabs of metal, plants like randomly scattered rocks; the liquefied air forms into solid pieces of ice, newspapers turn murderous, laughter disappears without a trace, and faces are covered with cold. Hearts lose their blood color and harden like stones.

Everything started on July 1. What a beautiful, solemn day was July 1—a day that fired us with enthu-

3

siasm. Before this day, Zhong Yicheng, who was a
young cadre on P——'s Communist Party Central District Committee, and also team leader of the Investigative Research Office Team, was as he had always
been in the numerous post-liberation political movements—enthusiastic, impassioned, and totally without reserve as he joined in the anti-rightist struggle.
After all, he was a member of the three-man office
team leading the movement. Then, on July 1, a newspaper in the capital ran an article by a new star of
literary criticism circles. It criticized a short poem
Zhong Yicheng had published in a very small children's picture book. The poem, entitled "Little Winter
Wheat Tells Its Tale," was only four lines in all:

> When wild chrysanthemums wilt,
> We start to come up;
> When frozen snow covers the ground,
> We are full of harvest's seeds.

Poor Zhong Yicheng had come to love poetry. (Some
people say poets never come to a good end. Byron,
Shelley, Pushkin, Mayakovsky—if they were not
killed in a fight, they committed suicide, or they were
locked up for having illicit affairs.) He read so much
poetry, and, tears flowing, chanted it aloud; he stayed
up all night, crying, laughing, mumbling, shouting.
He wrote so many poems, going over and over them
in a low voice. Originally the short poem "Little Win-

ter Wheat Tells Its Tale" was several lines longer, but some erudite, lofty, near-sighted editor chopped it down to four in the end. These four lines were the only poetry Zhong Yicheng had published, and even they were just printed in the lower righthand corner of a country scene. Still, it was a glorious and happy thing. The picture showed a great expanse of land alive with quivering yellow chrysanthemums, a sky filled with white snow, green sprouts like a patch of bright felt, and heavy ears of wheat . . . These four lines had so much of his love and dreams stored up inside them. He was speaking to thousands and thousands of children. After reading his poem, a fat little boy dressed like a sailor asked his mother, "What is 'little wheat'? How much smaller is it than 'big wheat'?" "Sweetie, little doesn't really mean little, don't you see?" His curly-haired mother laughed, not knowing which words to choose. A girl with long braids read his four-line poem and wanted to go to the country to see the fields, the peasants and farmers, the cycle of the crops, and the mill where wheat turned into snow-white flour . . . What a marvelous thing!

Then he was criticized by the new star of literary criticism. This new star was just coming into his own. The title of his piece was "What Tale Is He Telling?" He said this poem had been published in May 1957, just when the anti-Party and anti-socialist ultra-rightist elements were recklessly attacking the Party and shouting, "Get off the stage," "Get out of the way," and "Kill the Communist Party." They were using every available method, including writing poetry, to spew forth their bloodcurdling hatred for the Party and the people, their illusory hopes of changing the world, and their thirst for retaliation. Therefore one must analyze "Little Winter Wheat Tells Its Tale" from the viewpoint of political struggle; one must not lower one's guard and be fooled by a wolf in lamb's clothing or a poisonous snake in the guise of a beautiful woman. "When wild chrysanthemums wilt" meant the Communist Party should step down. Calling the Party "wild" was exactly what Austin, the American representative to the United Nations, did when he accused the Party of destroying civilization. "We start to come up" meant the tenacious capitalist and rightist cliques would take power. "We" was the Zhang-Luo Alliance; "we" were Huang Shiren, Mu Renzhi, Chiang Kai-shek, and Song Meiling.[1] In the line "When frozen snow covers the ground" one could

1. Warren Robinson Austin (1877–1962) was U.S. representative to the United Nations from 1946 to 1953. The Zhang-Luo Alliance refers to Zhang Bojun (1895–) and Luo Longji (1896–1965), who allegedly organized a group to attack the Communist Party. In 1957 they were branded as the worst "rightist elements" of China. Song Meiling (1897–) is Chiang Kai-shek's wife. Huang Shiren and Mu Renzhi are both characters in the revolutionary opera "The White-Haired Girl," written collectively at the Lu Xun Academy of the Arts in Yan'an in 1945. Huang is a typical feudal landlord, and Mu is his lackey.

clearly hear the reactionaries grinding their teeth in great gloom, fear, and hostility as they thought of destroying our socialism and the dictatorship of the proletariat. But the author's hidden allusions didn't stop here. "We are full of harvest's seeds" was in fact an open call to get on with the counter-revolutionary rebellion.

The newspaper that carried this article did not arrive in P—— until the afternoon, and it reached the Central District Committee just as workers got off. It was like a bomb exploding; some people were shocked, some were afraid, some were anxious, and some were excited. Zhong Yicheng read just a few lines and let out a yelp. He stuttered and stammered and his face grew hot, but the star of criticism had pinned his arms behind him and was taking shots from both sides. Why didn't you ask who I was? How can you show me to be like this without knowing anything about my political history and actual performance? Zong Yicheng wanted to fight back, but he couldn't get anything out—the star had already throttled him. The star's sense of principle was so strong, his questions were so piercing, bold, and high-principled, and his arguments were irrefutable, like a hot knife cutting through butter. The charges were so serious and demanding of attention that they possessed the power to shatter any defense. There was something about the article that precluded all discussion. One could disagree with literary criticism, but political judgments were like death sentences handed down by a military court; on the spot execution was the only response.

But he couldn't accept it; he had to fight back. If a car had charged along the sidewalk into a department store or a hefty thief grabbed an ax and run around terrorizing young girls in broad daylight, if someone had dug a ninety-foot hole and shoved a big building into it or, clutching an automatic rifle, scattered bullets into a grade-school classroom, probably none of these things could have shaken Zhong Yicheng more than this critical essay. Right there in black and white, undeniable facts, but how could our own newspaper publish such outrageous lies? Did all of that frightening analysis really apply to his little poem? He heard his bones crack as the star of criticism rolled him up and bit into him, first with his front teeth, then his incisors, finally chewing him up with his molars.

He went to find the District Committee Secretary, Wei. Wei lived in the courtyard behind the District Committee Office. His wife worked in this office too, but Wei seemed almost to live there. As he read the newspaper under the lamplight, Wei's eyebrows knit together tightly; he didn't wait for Zhong Yicheng to finish his impassioned plea, but told him, "Take it easy, control yourself. You have to hang on. Just keep working hard! Of course we can talk it over if you want to, just come by."

The District Committee Secretary's words, and especially his attitude, put Zhong Yicheng at ease. But when he walked down the hall past the office, he happened to catch sight of the office chairman and leader of the three-man team, Song Ming, clutching a red pencil, engrossed in reading and making notes all over the critical essay. He didn't know why, but he felt a little apprehension when he saw Song Ming. Song's small face was covered with wrinkles like an old man's, but his glasses were tiny, like those of a small child. He and his wife had just recently been divorced. Song Ming walked around all day with a grave countenance, and it seemed as if the only language he knew was that of newspapers and documents. Something that had once made a deep impression on Zhong Yicheng was his discovery of rows of dense writing on Song Ming's desk calendar: "speed up ——— report," "report ——— quantity," "reply to ——— news report," "get ——— name list," and also "went to movies with Shu Qin and chatted together" (Shu Qin was his wife's name—at that time, of course, they were not yet divorced), and "came around to tell Ah Xiong lies" (Ah Xiong was his son, now six years old). Now, with the star's essay, Zhong Yicheng felt there surely would be a new item on the calendar, something like "think over Zhong Yicheng's poem, 'Tells Its Tale.'" It gave him goosebumps.

Zhong Yicheng went to find his girlfriend, Ling Xue. She said, "He's just trying to make you into something you're not! It's obviously just conspiracy and slander; it's ridiculous! Just because he says something doesn't make it so; don't pay any attention to him! Don't worry. Let's go out and have something cold to drink."

Zhong Yicheng was touched by her words. He looked up and saw that the sky had not yet fallen, and stamping his feet, felt that the earth beneath them had not yet caved in. Zhong Yicheng was still Zhong Yicheng, love was still love, and the District Committee was still the District Committee. But he felt Ling Xue had looked at the problem too simplistically. She had not understood that behind the aggressive stance and words of the new star lurked a great danger.

What danger? He didn't dare think about it. He could imagine his life's end, or even the demise and death of the solar system, but he could not visualize what this danger was. From July 1 on, however, he developed a vexing and humiliating state of mind. He watched the eyes and faces of those around him, extremely conscious of their attitudes toward him. Maybe his nerves were excessively overwrought, or maybe he really had reason to feel this way, but he noticed that after that day almost everyone's attitude more or less changed—he knew it was because of the star's essay. Some people smiled as usual when they saw him, but before their smile was complete it would be withdrawn. This sort of odd facial activity made him miserable. Some people reached to shake his hand as they used to, but shook it quickly with their eyes elsewhere. Some of his best friends would have been embarrassed to ignore him, so they said a few words, but their awkwardness clearly showed their distraction. Only Song Ming had not changed—in fact, his attitude toward him seemed even better than before. Song Ming's courteous face conveyed a kind of self-esteem, a kind of satisfaction, but not a trace of hypocrisy.

In August, the situation changed radically. First the higher-ups criticized the district's anti-rightist movement for being excessive in three areas and deficient in three others. They said the district made a lot of noise about rightists, but hardly ever identified them, and the ones the district did pull out came from the ranks of pre-liberation personnel who used to work for the old regime, and seldom from the revolutionary ranks or, especially, the Party. Furthermore, the rightists came from the grassroots level rather than from among the leaders of the District Committee. After this Song Ming took the offensive at every meeting and put up posters blaming Wei's weakness and leniency, as well as the general rightist tendencies of the other leaders, for the district's lethargy in getting on with the movement. How could they possibly lead an anti-rightist movement? For example, a newspaper in the capital had already severely criticized Zhong Yicheng's anti-Party poetry, but the District Committee just sat there, letting Zhong lurk around as one of the three-man team. Didn't this show how

low Wei's political acumen had sunk? So naturally,
under the attack of Song Ming and the higher-ups,
Wei made one self-criticism after another, and Zhong
Yicheng was transferred out of the three-man team.
Right after this, the movement entered a new phase
in every department; rightists were tumbled out in
every direction. Posters exposing Zhong Yicheng
started appearing everywhere. Isn't it strange that as
soon as an admirable person is exposed, his whole
body suddenly seems covered with scabs? Zhong
Yicheng once ridiculed a certain leader for his verbosity . . . Zhong Yicheng once said this or that document, bulletin, or data was useless . . . Zhong Yicheng said there were problems in the relationship
between the Party and the people . . . More and more,
until Zhong Yicheng himself was totally confused. Finally, on this strangely hot day, he was called in for a
talk. The main leader talking to him was Song Ming,
and Wei was also present.

   This began a new phase of his life; any continuity he
had once possessed was shattered.

June 1966

   Fiery red armbands set flames to young hearts. Re-
sounding quotations urged children to fight. Charge,
fight, smash, go out with red in your eyes and build a

red, red world. But they still didn't know who their opponents were.

Still there were labels. Because he had been labeled, Zhong Yicheng was interrogated:

"Answer: you hate the Party, don't you? What kind of dreams do you dream about recovering your lost paradise?"

"Answer: what kind of anti-revolutionary plots have you hatched? How are you now preparing to overthrow the Party?"

"Answer: what kind of old documents have you kept, hoping to get back all your old property? You want Chiang Kai-shek to come back to power so you can get revenge and kill off the Party, don't you?"

Everyone chanted these questions together:

"When the enemies with guns are extinguished, those without guns still remain . . ."

"Revolution is not a dinner party, or writing essays . . ."[2]

A leather belt snapped, a chain clanked, and an anguished cry rang out.

"Answer, answer, answer!"

"I love the Party!"

"Bullshit! How could you love the Party? How could you possibly love the Party? How dare you say you

2. These quotes are from speeches of Mao Zedong during the Cultural Revolution.

love the Party? How could you deserve to love the Party? You're a stubborn mule with a head of granite! You're trying to provoke the Party! You won't admit defeat or confess to your crimes—you want to fight back as hard as you can! We're going to turn you upside down and trample you . . ."

Swish, clank, belt and chain, fire and ice, blood and sweat. Zhong Yicheng lost consciousness, but just at that instant he saw everything in a flash—forever fresh, forever alive, forever sacred, and not far away at all.

II

January 1949

On January 11, 1949, the People's Liberation Army launched a general offensive toward P——. After two days, P——'s Underground Party Committee notified all secret branches: the decisive moment had arrived. In order to prevent the Nationalist forces from taking reckless advantage of the chaos, and local toughs and other social dregs from utilizing the blank page between the chapters of the old and the new to plunder and otherwise break the law, all branches must bring in the People's Liberation Army immediately according to deployment plans worked out carefully over the last two months.

After receiving instructions from his superiors, Zhong Yicheng, who was then a seventeen-year-old high-school student in the P—— Provincial Number One High School and the branch secretary of one of three equally important branches, and who had been an alternate Party member for two-and-a-half years, broke with the routine of secret work and that same night gathered together four Party members he had worked with (including one mathematics professor over fifty years old) and thirteen Alliance members. They met in a long-unused underground boiler room. In the dim glow of a candle (the electricity plants had

15

stopped working long ago) he read the instructions from the Party superiors and in a crisp, precise voice delegated responsibility among the seventeen people. At the first meeting, the seventeen people expressed confidence and pride in the great enthusiasm of the Party and Alliance members, and in their capable, experienced, intelligent and selfless leader, Zhong Yicheng. It was deep midnight when they returned to the dormitory; they woke up all the students in the north wing, and Zhong Yicheng told them:

"Fellow students, the People's Liberation Army has already fought its way into the city, and the evil rule of the reactionary Nationalist clique is over! China's thousands of years of man-eating history have come to an end! The sky is bright! Flourishing, strong, prosperous, free, and equal—new China, with the people as master, is about to be born! As the Student Alliance of Northern China has requested, we will organize units to guard the school and the city, to prevent destruction, to preserve scenic and historic spots and the lives and property of the people. Anyone who wants to participate come over here and get an armband."

As Zhong Yicheng produced the pennants and armbands of the Student Alliance, which had been prepared long before, the students' faces showed pleasant surprise, astonishment, and perplexity. There had been a few among the students who were spies or escaped relatives of the reactionary landlords in the liberated areas, but not long ago the "general suppression" had recruited them for the "Self-Salvation Vanguard," which was preparing for a death struggle with the Communist Party. Almost all of the students remaining in the dorms were on the correct side. In a short time, as the secret Party and Alliance members spurred them on, all but the most cowardly and vacillating students responded to these proud words: "Our country's life or death depends on you! . . . We are the masters of a new era, the pioneers of a new society!" They put on red armbands and pried open the door to the physical education storeroom (no one knew where the school administrators had gone) where each person clasped a "boy scout" army stick as a weapon and filed out of the school. To guard the school, a teacher who was a Party member organized a group of teachers and staff under the title of the already existing Teachers' Alliance.

The sky lightened faintly, and in the chilly wind the sound of exploding bombs ceased. Guns still sounded, sometimes in quick volleys and sometimes shot by shot. A sound like the popping of corn came from far away, while close by bullets cut through the air with a sharp crack. The smell of smoke filled the air. The streets were quiet and not a soul was to be seen. All the stores had tightly closed their doors and windows and covered them with thick, heavy slabs of wood. The few remaining noisy, old streetcars and rebuilt wood-burning buses that usually ran along the road spouting out noxious smoke were nowhere to be seen. The rickshaws, pedicabs, and pushcarts had also disappeared without a trace. Even the one and only thing that seemed to grow and expand at great speed in this daily shrinking and weakening town—the corps of beggars—had somehow disappeared. Only the piles of multi-colored rubbish scattered around the street could make one think of the city's inhabitants and their lives; decaying, dying, degenerating, and yet also transforming and soon to be reborn.

Zhong Yicheng led a group of over thirty young high-school students by. The oldest among them was twenty-one, the youngest fourteen, and they averaged under eighteen. Their clothes were ragged and the tips of their ears and noses were red with cold, but their faces were serious yet excited, naive and curious yet solemn and brave. They stood with their backs straight and walked with big strides; their gaze was bright and piercing, and their hearts were filled with a pride only to be understood by those who themselves had set the wheels of history turning.

> We are the ones who cleared the way.
> We are the ones who chopped the trees.
> We built the house that reached the sky.
> We are strong and brave with naught to fear.
> Our iron backs destroy the old world.
> We build a new world,
> We build a new world!

It seemed as if Zhong Yicheng could hear the strong strains of this favorite song in his ears. "Tighten up! . . . Stand straight! . . . Left march!" Zhong Yicheng's manner was stern as he directed the unit to the stone bridge on the Jinpo River, where they were supposed to stand guard. As they neared this ancient stone bridge, which strategically linked the east and west banks of the river, a unit from the girls' high school approached from the south side of the intersection. In old, tattered clothes, faces yellow and gaunt, they looked like the unhealthy trees and shrubs that grow on a barren mountain slope. But each one of them glowed with vigor, and they moved with speed and precision, just like a well-trained unit. Zhong Yicheng immediately recognized their unit leader—Ling Xue.

Ling Xue was a third-year student at Jingzhen High School, a private school for girls. She had a round face, a narrow forehead, and short hair; her eyes were very deep, calm, and gentle. Her shiny nose was graceful and regular, with an air of cockiness about it; her mouth was often tightly closed but still carried the hint of a smile. They had met and talked before, once in 1947 at a campfire meeting where autonomous alliances of students from five universities had organized a cooperative to fight the civil war and starvation, once in 1948 in a parade to protest a massacre of students by the bogus congress in the northwest, and

later at movies sponsored by the Soviet Union Cross-Cultural Association. Today, their unexpected meeting on the streets of a city that was soon to belong to the people, at this historical pivot point, with both of them unit leaders, was a public pronouncement of their political convictions. On both of their faces were understanding smiles; their hearts were warmed by a revolutionary fervor that brought them closer than brother and sister or husband and wife. "The sky is bright!" Zhong Yicheng raised his hand and shouted to Ling Xue.

Just as Ling Xue was about to respond to Zhong Yicheng's greeting, a volley of shots rang out. Two soldiers from the Nationalist Party's defeated ranks fled in panic along the dried-up riverbed. One of them had an obvious wound on his leg; the green bandage wrapped around it was stained red, and he limped. The other, a tall man with a beard covering his face, carried a rifle; he looked like a demon. Zhong Yicheng jumped off the six-foot-high bridge onto the tall man, and they both fell to the ground. When he caught a whiff of the pungent, moldy smell of the man's body, Zhong Yicheng raised his stick and called out, "Put down your guns and put up your hands!" The students, boys and girls alike, all rushed over and encircled them.

The two soldiers hurriedly raised their hands, the lame one kneeling on the ground. They had not considered resisting, and indeed they could not have resisted; in the same way, the young students had not considered the danger to them, and indeed there was very little—the revolution was victorious and so were they. Not even Zhong Yicheng, who had leapt six feet down, had hurt himself; his skin wasn't even scratched. "Take them over there!" He gave orders like a field sergeant.

"Congratulations! As soon as you show up, success is ours!" Ling Xue came over laughing and shook Zhong Yicheng's hand just like an adult. Then she gathered her unit together and went on.

What are you responsible for?" Zhong Yicheng asked them from behind.

"The drum tower." As Ling Xue turned her head to answer, she raised her left fist high, and waving it at Zhong Yicheng, yelled,

"Bolshevik salute!"

What? Bolshevik salute? That meant the salute of the Bolsheviks—the Communist Party members' salute! Zhong Yicheng had heard that, in the liberated areas, people in the Party organizations and institutions sometimes used these two words as a greeting on paper, but this was the first time he had heard it in real life, from a young living comrade like himself. It was a fiery word, a greeting that filled him with joy. Bolshevik salute! Bolshevik salute! The melodious sound resounded in his ears . . .

June 1966

He woke up with a start.

He looked at the young people with red armbands. Green military uniforms, wide belts, two little braids like the horns on a goat, sleeves halfway rolled up . . . how old could they be? Like me in 1949, about seventeen? Seventeen was really an age for revolution, an age to wear armbands! Except for cowards, idiots, and otherwise hopeless parasites, what seventeen-year-old did not want to blow away the foundations of the old society with bombs and detonators, or dispose of all the filth and human weakness of history and build a bright, new, just world with fresh red flags, armbands, and fiery poetry? Who did not want to topple mountains into the sea, radically turn the tides, and in one morning destroy all selfishness, falseness, and injustice? Seventeen was an age of great fervor, purity, and joy! In the eternally forward movement of human history, seventeen-year-olds were so important. If there were no seventeen-year-olds, there would be no progress, no development, and certainly no revolution.

"My dear little revolutionary generals," he mumbled.

"Bullshit! Shut your dog's mouth, don't try to get in good with us!"

Another round of pain and fainting. Why was it so hot, did it mean they were going to build a fire and put him in it? Could it be that they had thrown gasoline on his body and were going to light him on fire? Their enthusiasm, their willingness to give their lives, their belief in the slogans of revolution—they could have used these things so well!

"Bolshevik salute!" As he lost consciousness once again, the bloody corners of his mouth carried a hint of his heart's smile, and he suddenly shouted out these words.

"What? What did he say? Bullshit? Bullshit who? Who would this scabby dog dare shit on?"

"No no, I heard him say *burashito;* it's probably Japanese. Maybe it's a contact's code word—do you think he's a Japanese spy?"

"Report: he hasn't regained consciousness. Is he—dead?"

"Don't panic. An enemy. A scabby dog. The revolution commits no crimes; rebellion is justified!"

March 1970

In the "purify the class ranks" study group. The assistant group leader sported a black beard, recently grown, a cigarette dangling from his mouth, and half-closed eyes; mumbling his words together (he thought his thick-tongued stutter, hoarse voice, and ungrammatical language showed him to be an old hand with high qualifications), he spoke to Zhong Yicheng:

"Your history is one of fabrication from top to bottom. You're not telling the truth. Your problem is very serious. People like you have more than enough qualifications for us to send you to the Public Security Special Division. Some not as bad as you have been executed. You yourself know for sure what sleazy bastards you all are. You entered the Party at fifteen and were an alternate member branch secretary at seventeen—who do you think you're kidding? Did you fill out a form? Who approved you? What oath did you take? Why was there only one person who recommended you . . . ?"

"That was the underground, special conditions . . ."

"What special conditions! It looks like a fake Communist Party to me!"

"You can't say that, sir, you can't say that!"

"Tell the truth!"

"I . . ."

"We beat the Japanese invaders, we destroyed Chiang Kai-shek's central forces of eight million. You're just one little Zhong Yicheng and you still don't dare tell us the truth?"

III

This was a town nearing death. Of its ancient history, its long civilization, and its flourishing past, only a gray shadow remained. What was piled before one's eyes in the streets and alleys, all the way up to the entrance of the busiest streets, was garbage. The children of the poor scrounged around in trash piles all day, using specially made claws of coarse iron wires to rake around and dig up some treasure they could pick out—a bit of coal not totally burnt, some vegetable leaves, some bean skins or a fish head swarming with countless flies. The newspaper had run several such stories as "Thirteen Persons, Old and Young, All Perish," telling how an entire poor family had died from eating rotten fish heads, but the children of the poor still saw them as treasures. "My good gentlemen and ladies, if you have some left over give me a bite!" Everywhere these gently plaintive, miserable wails had become the main melodies of the city. Along with this was the common chorus of the policeman's whistle, the sounds of arguments and fights, hoarse voices selling medicine made from monkeys, and the mating calls of hundreds and thousands of motley cats and dogs, their tails between their legs. Three-year-old children sang "This kind of woman's an atomic bomb," twenty-year-old boys sang "My heart is in two

25

big pieces." . . . In the winter, totally naked beggars would take up pieces of bricks and purposely beat them against their sunken chests, hoping to stir people's sympathy; others would just take a knife and sever the veins in their faces, smearing themselves red with blood. And right next to them, fat, robust officials and rich businessmen came out of the glistening glass doors of the famous restaurant *Pavilion of Delicacies* with red-lipped, fur-clothed women on their arms . . .

But even in this decaying body that spewed out disgusting fumes, a new, healthy life-force was generating: the Party, its underground organizations, its many underground members, and its offshoots, the members of the Democratic Youth Alliance. In the enemy's heartland, under the sharp knives of the law-enforcement groups jointly organized by the armed forces, military police, and civilian police corps to wipe out the "communist spies" on the spot, in jails, right next to the clubs carried by police, and on the torture rack, they went on with their revolutionary activities. Among those working with the People's Liberation Army were many young people, several the age of Zhong Yicheng, and also some even younger, serious children. They were children; they went free of bias to be molded by life, the great teacher. The first lessons they had in this world were of hunger, poverty, oppression, degradation, and fear, so what they learned was naturally hatred and struggle. In the cities, the Party's work—the work of the underground cadres—lit the torches of revolutionary truth in the spirit of these children and their consuming hatred and desire to fight back. At first they used the works of Zou Taofen and Ai Siqi and social science pamphlets published by the New Knowledge Bookstore, Life's Bookstore, and the Reader's Publishing Company, as well as progressive publications from Hong Kong and Shanghai, to inspire the minds of the young people and help them see the truth.[3] These writings let them hear another strong sound that was one with the hearts of the people and called them to struggle for their own freedom and happiness. Then the cadres went one step further. Wedged in under the cover of *The Travels of Lao Can* or *Gold-Powdered Aristocrats* the children would find Xinhua News Agency dispatches, Beijing Broadcasting news reports, outlines of land reform programs, and even "Discussion on Coalition Government" and "On New Democracy."[4] So when they grew older and

3. Zou Taofen (1895–1944), a reporter, politician, theorist, and publisher who opposed the Nationalist Party, started the Life Bookstore *(Shenghuo shudian)* in 1932. Zou was posthumously made a member of the Communist Party. Ai Siqi (1910–66) was a Communist Party philosopher and theorist.

4. *The Travels of Lao Can,* a novel by Liu E (1857–1909), and *Gold-Powdered Aristocrats,* a novel by Zhang Henshui (1895–1967), are both considered non-political reading, as opposed to "Discussion on Coalition Government" (1945) and "On New Democracy" (1940) by Mao Zedong.

became serious, they were conscious of a desire to use
all their strength to send the old monarchy to its
grave and create a new world. They gravely considered the danger they faced in their revolutionary activities, but they were prepared to sacrifice and determined to sacrifice. They entered the Party before they
reached eighteen (Zhong Yicheng entered at just
fifteen). Because of the particular features of espio-
nage work, within one unit there were several secret
branches unknown to each other. Only when there are
many such parallel branches are they difficult to ex-
pose. Thus the Party's organizations developed rapidly, to the point where alternate Party members
were all Party secretaries. They were still children;
their understanding of the Party and the revolution
could not avoid being superficial and immature. But
they stood firm and feared nothing; they were serious,
responsible Party members.

Three days after the fight to liberate P——— was
over, Zhong Yicheng received a notice to go to the
main hall at S——— University for a city-wide meeting
of Party members. The weather was freezing cold.
Zhong Yicheng's jacket, already too small, was the
one his mother had made for him four years before
when he was thirteen. His blue-cold hands and wrists
hung outside, and the armpits were so tight that he
couldn't move. His legs warded off the cold with a
worn pair of sweat pants on which the threads were
all matted together. Except for a beat-up ballpoint

pen and a small notebook in the pocket of his jacket, he didn't look any different from the beggars lining the streets or the children climbing on trash piles and picking out pieces of coal. But his thick, short eyebrows arched like wings wanting to fly, his face showed a deep joy and pride straight from the heart, and his movements were quick and full of confidence: We have won, we are already the all-powerful masters of this city and all of China. He walked along the city's streets, saw the dilapidated walls and old houses along the road, and thought: We must turn this upside down. He also saw one military truck after another rushing to ship the trash away. When the fighting had stopped, the military trucks would launch into a morning-and-night, twenty-four-hour-a-day, continuous battle to get rid of this trash. Soon all the filth would have thoroughly disappeared without a speck. P——'s garbage problem, three times previously discussed and decided on by the Nationalists' bogus congress, many times the cause of "special donations" and a "special sanitary fee," and again and again investigated by the bogus government's investigative bureau, had finally swallowed up the city, just as the government officials swallowed up the special fee. But now, the garbage was breathing its last and had lost its overwhelming prestige and power. This, Zhong Yicheng thought, is because we have destroyed it. He also saw a few bone-thin children all alone, cowering and shivering in the cold wind. Don't worry, we'll turn you into civilized, fortunate, healthy, and useful human material. As he neared S—— University, he saw soldiers with the words "People's Liberation Army" on their chests, and "P—— Garrison Command" on their arms. He stood leisurely at a distance and got out the red entry permit his superiors had given him, waved it at them and said, "I am a Party member." That entry permit could talk; it said respectfully to the soldiers, "Bolshevik salute!" The soldiers replied to the young secret Party member with a small smile that also indicated respect: "We've joined forces." Those smiling faces said, "Because of you, we are not afraid of being captured or massacred anymore!" Zhong Yicheng returned a moved, smiling countenance. What was the topic of the meeting this time? As he approached the meeting hall, Zhong Yicheng wondered if after the meeting they would organize a group to go to Taiwan. They should know we are experienced workers, and our age suits us even more for hidden and clandestine activities. We could see the sharp knives of the Nationalist armed forces, military and civilian police, and talk to the Central Committee Control as well . . . That would be even more glorious. I'll be the first to sign up.

He walked into the hall, and instantly taken aback, stood dumbfounded.

So there were so many Communist Party members, a dense mass of them, up to a thousand! There were

two million people in P——; in later days, when the
Communist Party was openly the governing party,
one thousand Party members would not be much, but
before liberation, right under the enemy's nose, each
Party member was a sword, a lantern, a sower of
seeds, and a torch in the vast expanse of darkness.
Cultivating a Party member did not just mean taking
the enemy's strongholds and building one's own fort.
In the months and years of harsh, cruel struggle, each
Party member was so precious and necessary! Zhong
Yicheng, who was used to one-way contacts, had met
no Party members other than one superior and four
branch members (these four Party members had not
known each other four days before). How could one
not gasp in amazement at seeing such a huge number
of the ranks sitting upright and proper in the meeting
hall? He was like a child used to rowing a rubber raft
in a ditch who suddenly finds himself on a big ship
heading out in high waves and wild winds to the huge
sea beyond.

And how the strong sad song raged in his ears:

> Arise, ye prisoners of starvation,
> Arise, ye wretched of the earth . . .

A man wearing an army uniform (of course he was
a Party member!) was waving his arms broadly, beating out the rhythm and teaching everyone to sing

"The Internationale." In the past, Zhong Yicheng had only seen this song described in Soviet novels, when Bolsheviks were martyred.

> Quickly burn the torch red,
> Strike when the iron is hot . . .

These lyrics, this melody, these hundreds and thousands of starving, cold slaves—criminals not worth a cent—the chorus of the Communist Party members, strike when the iron is hot, these words made Zhong Yicheng's blood race. He never before had heard such a majestically sad, noble, emotion-filled song. Hearing this song made one want to parade down the street scattering leaflets, tear down the jails and the locks and chains, take up knives and guns and start an armed insurrection, rush in and attack the last stubborn fortress of the old world . . . Zhong Yicheng clenched his fists, his eyes filled with hot tears. Through his blurry tears, the two red hammer-and-sickle Party flags hanging on the stage and the huge portrait of Party leader Mao Zedong between them looked even larger and more dazzling.

Actually the hall was run down. The roof had no ceiling—the girders and crossbeams were all exposed. Many window frames were crooked and bent, the broken parts nailed over the pieces of wood or even closed up with a wall of bricks. Under the chairman's stage were two Texaco oil barrels being used as

stoves, but because the coal in them was of poor quality and their smokestacks leaked air, they filled the
hall with smoke that made the eyes smart. All this
notwithstanding, under the huge blood-red high-
flying Party flag, the lofty, glorious, benevolent picture of Chairman Mao, the heroic, magnificent, moving strains of "The Internationale," the meeting hall
already had taken on a new significance and charm.
The Party's brilliance had changed this run-down au-
ditorium into a place of majestic beauty and strength.

The commanding officers of the field operation that
liberated P———, as well as the political commissars,
the first and second secretaries of the Municipal Party
Committee, newly enriched from the foundations of
the underground Municipal Party Committee, those in
charge of the original underground Education Committee, Labor Committee, and Agriculture Committee, and the chairman and assistant chairman of the
People's Liberation Army military control unit, which
had been organized long before the fighting had
started and had liberated P———, all filled the stage.
They wore grass-green military uniforms or gray
cadre uniforms which had been mass-produced and did
not fit them well at all. Because they had never paid
much attention to washing or ironing, their clothes all
looked wrinkled. Each one of them was travel-weary
and had very bloodshot eyes from staying up all night.
The oldest among them was not over fifty; most were
in their thirties or forties; and some leaders had just

turned twenty. (In Zhong Yicheng's eyes they were already elders of noble character and high prestige.) They all had nimble bodies, great agility, and abounding energy; none were fat, aged, rigid or slow. They were more spirited than the average, but aside from that their outward appearance did not set them apart from others. Nevertheless, Zhong Yicheng was familiar with their names. The names of several of the generals among them had appeared in Nationalist newspapers more than once. These gossip papers printed the thoroughly ridiculous news, a product of their wishful thinking, that these military leaders had been "shot dead." Now these generals who had been "shot dead" in the Nationalist newspapers played the roles of victors, liberators, and leaders on the lecture stage of P——, where the wartime smoke had just cleared. Facing the defenders of the second front line, they began to speak.

The leaders reported one after another. Hunan accents, Sichuan accents, Shanxi accents, and Dongbei accents. They talked about the war situation, future developments and hopes, the Nationalists' destruction of P——, the difficulties before them and how to solve them. . . . Each leader spoke with clarity and lucidity; forthright, logical, confident, surging with enthusiasm and strength, their analyses were precise and their plans astute. They were as infectiously excited as a line of fire spreading out, and at the same time they moved in steps as prescribed as those of an accountant figuring his accounts. Naturally there was none of yesterday's empty, weak wail, so recently passed away; the hackneyed old terms of officialese, the rotten inflections of extreme corruption, the empty claptrap designed to get sympathy, or the devilish words that straddled the fence. These were no longer words muttered secretly under one's breath, nor secretly transmitted codes or hidden allusions, documents, or orders. It was the Party's will being loudly proclaimed, the Party's strategy in great detail and clearly delineated—the sound of the Party. Zhong Yicheng soaked up the Party's wisdom and strength like a sponge. He was enthusiastic and delighted; he prostrated himself before this totally new way of thinking and speaking, these new concepts and this new language. With each new sentence it was as if he had learned something new, had grown bigger and taller and a bit more mature.

Before he knew it, darkness came. Who knew how much time had passed? The lights came on. Very fortunately, because the plant protection unit of underground Party workers had guarded the electricity plant, the generator facilities had totally escaped harm. Moreover, forty-eight hours after the fighting had stopped, the electricity, which had been off for over a month, came back on. What bright lights, what a great city! But as the lights came on, Zhong Yicheng abruptly perceived something else: hunger.

Of course. He had rushed to the meeting at noon

and had not had time to eat, so he had just bought two scoops of shelled peanuts in the store. How could he not be hungry at this late hour!

As if to respond to him, the Vice Chairman of Military Affairs, who was presiding over this meeting, interrupted the speech being given by the leader of the Municipal Committee to say that the last summary speech, to be delivered by the First Secretary of the Municipal Committee, would be quite long—three hours, he estimated. In order to resolve the contradictions of the stomach, they had sent two jeeps, which had already returned with food, so they would take a break and have dinner.

Thus the entire hall was filled with flatbread stuffed with meat, rolls full of strips of deep-fried dough, bread twists and doughnuts, grit bread stuffed with spicy, salty vegetables, and fried eggs wrapped in biscuits. Baskets, straw purses, trays, bags—a motley assortment of utensils brought a motley assortment of provisions from the shelves of private stores. To look at them it seemed as if they had bought out several neighborhood stores. Zhong Yicheng's seat was next to the aisle, and his mouth watered greedily as he looked at this food. To a poverty-stricken person like him, even flatbread and strips of deep-fried dough were treasures he could not take lightly. He did not worry about eating himself, but happily passed flatbread and deep-fried dough strips to the People's Liberation Army comrades (the workers of the meeting).

He stood a ways away and tossed the food over with great accuracy. All kinds of plain but tasty food flew over the heads of the city's Party members, who had fought their way from the underground to liberation. Laughter and shouting—"Give me some!" "Look!" "Don't forget me!"—merged together into one happy sound. This large-scale, lively meeting was the first one the revolutionary and Party units had ever had in P——. More than any other feast, it would be etched into the memories of these Party members. As quick and rough as a soldier, as innocent and pure as a child, as affable and loving as a family together . . . communism would surely come to pass, communism would surely be realized.

But Zhong Yicheng was so excited that as soon as the food came into his hands he gave it to someone else, and it seemed that in his happy hand-to-hand transferring he didn't save any for himself. The third consecutive willow basket was empty, and a fourth was not on the way—the food had already all been distributed. Because of their hunger, and maybe because of their happiness, everyone had wolfed down the food as fast as wind scattering loose clouds. They had annihilated the food and were taking out their handkerchiefs to wipe off their mouths and hands, but Zhong Yicheng still felt hungry. The fragrance of sesame, bread, and meat was still wafting about, and his stomach had come up to his throat and was about to pop out of his body and leap over to a man with some flatbread in his hand who was chewing carefully and swallowing slowly.

Zhong Yicheng was in sorry straits. He began to feel his head swirl and his eyes get dizzy from hunger, but he was also very happy and joyful. Just then a hand came around from behind him. He could not see who it was, but he already could see the golden deep-fried dough strip wedged between flatbread and offered in the hand.

"Take it."

"You?"

It was Ling Xue. She said laughing, "I've been sitting not far behind you, but you just kept looking straight ahead. Then I saw you so happy like that, and thought to myself, he mustn't forget about his own share . . ."

"And you?"

"I've . . . already eaten."

This clearly was not so. After going back and forth for a while, the two of them split it. Zhong Yicheng felt a little shy and embarrassed, but also very grateful and fortunate. He was so delighted at every bite of flatbread that he looked comical. Ling Xue laughed.

A whistling sound came out of the microphone and everyone went back to their seats. Ling Xue went back to her seat too. Zhong Yicheng once again focused on the report. He didn't turn around, but he felt a pair of friendly revolutionary eyes behind him.

. . . An unknown amount of time had passed, it was

the middle of the night, the meeting was over, and big white snowflakes were falling outside. When Zhong Yicheng went outside, a military officer saw his ill-fitting little jacket and his skinny wrists sticking out of his sleeves, and said: "My little friend, aren't you cold?" The general spoke in a booming voice and at the same time took off his own brand new fuzzy-collared, padded military overcoat, warm from his body, and threw it over Zhong Yicheng. Then the happy people flowing by pulled Zhong Yicheng along before he even had time to thank him.

1957–79

In these last twenty years, Zhong Yicheng often thought of that meeting and the first time he saw the Party flag and that huge portrait of Mao Zedong. He thought of that first time he heard the national anthem; he thought of that dinner and the unfamiliar man, who later became District Secretary Wei, who had given him his padded overcoat. He thought of the Communist Party members who had greeted each other with the Bolshevik salute. These memories gradually faded away with the passing of time, finally coalescing into a brilliant, radiating ray of light. In these last twenty-some years, no matter how many painful, frightening things he had seen, no matter how many of his idols had lost their halos, how many truly precious things had been ridiculed and stomped on, how many naive and beautiful dreams had popped like soap bubbles, and no matter how much he himself had been doubted, wronged, insulted—still, when he thought of that meeting of Party members and his life in the Party from 1947 to 1957, he felt an incomparable sense of accomplishment and pride, and also the resoluteness of his convictions. Communism absolutely could come to pass; world unity absolutely was possible; a completely new life, filled with brightness and justice (with many contradictions and problems as always) absolutely could be and in the past had been realized. Blood, fervor, pain; the costly, tortuous road of revolution had not been taken in vain. At thirteen he had worked close to the Party underground, at fifteen entered the Party, at seventeen taken on the job of branch secretary, and at eighteen left school to work for the Party. The road he had chosen was the right one, and the convictions he had fought for were honorable. For these convictions, and to have been able to participate in that first meeting of all the city's Party members, he was willing to pay the cost of a life of hardship, of being misunderstood and wronged. Even if he died under the stigma of all kinds of evil deeds, if sweet little seventeen-year-old revolutionary generals whipped him to death with belts and chains, if he had to die by bullets shot under the name of the Party by his own comrades, his heart would still be full of light. He felt no remorse or sorrow, he harbored no personal grievances or disillusionment. No matter what had happened, he still had the glorious pride that comes from becoming a member of that great and responsible Party. Even if he saw more of the Party's dark side, and more samples of human weakness, he could not hide his confidence in the Party, in life, and in human beings. Thinking back on that meeting just once made up for everything. He wasn't an actor in a tragedy; he was strong and fortunate.

IV

Zhong Yicheng was going to Wei's lectures on the Party. On the day that he turned eighteen, the branch bureau advanced him to the status of regular Party member.

Wei had said in class:

"A Party member must be truly Bolshevik; he must assume the nature of the Party completely and purely; he must forget the self and throw himself into the revolutionary struggle. Through the aid of Party organizations, he must use the weapons of criticism and self-criticism to change his thinking and conquer his own personal selfishness, his desire to be a hero, his liberalism, his subjectivism, his greed for glory, his jealousy . . . and so on, all of which is a part of the consciousness of the petty bourgeois and exploiting classes.

". . . Take individualism, for example. The proletarian class has no individualism, because it owns nothing. What it has lost are locks and chains, but what it has gained is the world. To liberate itself, it must first liberate all of humanity. It is most selfless and full of foresight. But individualism is the world view of the few who have personal possessions, the exploiters. It arose from private property and the separation of classes . . . Individualism is totally incompatible with

42

the nature of the proletarian party . . . A strong in-
dividualist who is unwilling to change eventually will
go over to Chiang Kai-shek, Truman, Trotsky, or Bu-
charin . . ."

"Exactly! Exactly!" Zhong Yicheng practically
shouted. Individualism was filthy and disgusting, like
a rotting sore, like nose snot, like cockroaches, like
flies and maggots . . .

District Secretary Wei continued:

"A Communist Party member is the vanguard soldier of the proletariat, a person who has thrown off all
base individual ambition and lowly interests. He is the
bravest person, and he feels life's greatest good fortune is to give himself to Party work. He is the wisest,
because his heart is like a bright mirror untouched by
the dust of selfish gain. He has the greatest future,
because his intelligence and talent will be forged and
matured in the struggle of hundreds and thousands of
people. He has the greatest ideal—to realize communism all over the world. He has the greatest toler-
ance, and for the Party's benefit and the realization of
his mission willingly suffers humiliation. He has the
greatest dignity: 'Fierce-browed, I coolly defy a thousand pointing fingers.' He has the greatest modesty:
'Head bowed like a willing ox, I work for the children.'[5] He has the greatest happiness: every small

5. These lines, from a poem by Lu Xun (1884–1936), were widely
quoted by Mao Zedong.

step for the Party's progress brings him joy. He has the greatest fortitude and is not afraid to climb a mountain of swords or plunge into a sea of flames for the Party . . ."

When the class was over, Zhong Yicheng and Ling Xue left the hall together. Zhong Yicheng told her unhurriedly:

"The branch has already made me a regular Party member. It means a lot to me to hear Wei's lecture right at this time. Give me some advice—what should I work on? I'm already determined to conquer my . . . plans for individual heroics, and I'll take ten years to conquer my unproletarian class consciousness completely and become a Bolshevik, a real true proletarian vanguard soldier just like Wei said. Help me out, give me some advice!"

"What did you say, Zhong?" Ling Xue blinked her eyes, as if she had not understood his words. "I think being a real, true, qualified Party member means a lifetime of effort. Is ten years . . . enough?"

"Naturally you have to work hard at studying and transforming yourself all your life. But even if it's just a first step you always need a goal as to when Bolshevism should be realized. If ten years isn't enough, then fifteen years, sixteen years . . ."

November 1957

Seven years later, Zhong Yicheng was branded an anti-Party, anti-socialist, capitalist, rightist element.

He went through three months of re-education, an endless political, mental, and psychological process, the result of which had actually been determined long ago. It included Song Ming's patient, extensive, and well-intentioned reasoning and analysis. Zhong Yicheng's own relentless self-criticism became increasingly exhaustive and difficult to extricate himself from. At first people had no bad intentions, but during the exposure-criticism conducted in response to the Party's call, there were some who, in an effort to appear more revolutionary, screamed out the most inflammatory words possible. Later, because of Song Ming's all-consuming and profound analysis and Zhong Yicheng's self-criticism, which shocked even him when he heard it, and still more because of the climbing political temperature, this exposure and criticism turned into a merciless and devastating attack. Finally a conclusion was reached.

The process of being labeled a "rightist element" was just like a surgical operation. Zhong Yicheng had been linked to the Party vein to vein, nerve to nerve, bone to bone, and flesh to flesh. He had had this kind of flesh-and-blood relationship with his revolutionary comrades in arms, the young people and the masses. Zhong Yicheng had been a piece of flesh on the body of the Party. Now the "surgeons" Song Ming and the new star of literary criticism had examined this piece of flesh with a meter that fluctuated wildly according to the weather, and had determined that it had grown a terminal cancer. So they had taken up a surgical knife and carefully, delicately, and conscientiously cut it out and thrown it away. And after it was cut out and thrown away it didn't matter if the original diagnosis was corrected; even Zhong Yicheng, not to mention other people, saw this piece of bleeding meat thrown in the trash and could not help but turn his eyes away in revulsion and disgust.

As for Zhong Yicheng himself, this was heart surgery, because the Party, the revolution, and communism were his blood-red heart. They were gouging out his heart under the name of the Party. And because he loved, supported, trusted, respected, and followed the Party, he should also take up the knife and dig some out, or at least direct their cutting: "Cut in here, right here . . ."

When the operation was over and he saw in the mirror the pale white face of the man who had lost his heart, he . . .

What chaos and confusion! I am an "element"! I am an enemy! I am a traitor! I am a criminal! I am a jackal or a wolf! I am an evil devil! I am the brother of Huang Shiren, the cousin of Mu Renshi, the secret commando of Truman, Dulles, Chiang Kai-shek, and Chen Lifu. No, actually I performed a base function the spies of America and Chiang Kai-shek could not; I was the little Nagy of China.[6] I should be shot or beaten to death with rods; even dead I would be dog shit, shameful to humanity; I would become a mouthful of sticky spittle, a tuberculous germ . . .

Sitting in the trolley, I didn't look the ticket seller or the other riders in the eye, because each one of them should rightfully scorn and despise me. When I went into the post office and stuck a stamp printed with a design of Tian'anmen Square on an envelope, everything before me turned black and my hands trembled, because I was an "enemy" who had schemed to overthrow socialism, to overthrow the People's Republic of China, and to overturn the brilliant Tian'anmen Square, with its five-star red flag.

6. Chen Lifu (1900–), belonged to one of the four wealthiest families in pre-1949 China. He worked as director of the Investigation Division of the Nationalist Party in the late twenties and thirties. Imre Nagy (1896–1958), a high official in the Communist Party of Hungary, was prime minister from 1953 to 1955, when he introduced moderate reforms that promised more consumer goods, opened concentration camps, ended deportation, and allowed peasants to leave collective farms. In 1955 these policies were criticized as "right-wing deviationism," and Nagy was expelled from the Party; this was protested by intellectuals, and Nagy was readmitted in 1956 and reappointed as prime minister in October, 1956. Nagy was executed in 1958 because of his role in the Hungarian Incident of October 1956, when he attempted to opt out of the Warsaw Pact. This incident supposedly influenced Mao Zedong in his attempt to crack down on intellectuals in the Anti-Rightist Movement of 1957.

When I walked past the breakfast shop, I didn't dare go in and buy a bowl of soybean milk. How could I dare, how could I be worthy of eating soybeans planted by the masses of peasants and ground up by the masses of workers, who both deeply loved the Party and socialism? How could I drink the sweet, white soybean soup cooked, sweetened, and poured into the bowl by a shopkeeper who deeply loved the Party and socialism? I saw the news in the paper that the Bank of China had issued coins, and I saw how people happily and curiously rushed to collect the one-, two-, and five-cent nickel coins, save them, and pass them on for others to appreciate. They were happy at the country's economic prosperity, the superiority of socialism, the stability of prices, and the inherent value of the coins, which were both durable and beautiful. I too got hold of a five-cent coin, and I too enjoyed the national banner, five-star flag, Tian'anmen Square, the heads of wheat, and the date. I loved it so much I couldn't let it go . . . but suddenly I caught sight of my own lousy dog's image in the reflection on the coin . . . What qualifications or rights did I have to delight in and applaud socialism or China's economic accomplishments? Wasn't I an enemy of the Republic, a devourer of socialism? Weren't the contradictions between me and my country irreconcilable, of opposite nature, contradictions between enemies that meant death for one of us? Wasn't it true that if I, this disgusting thing, had not been ferreted out and beaten down, I would have destroyed the People's Republic of China? Couldn't I be companion only to traitors, spies, and thieves who sold out their country? How could traitors, spies, and thieves who sold their country delight in coins issued by the People's Republic of China?

Alas, Chairman Mao, what does this all mean? What's really happening? Is this all real? Is it real?

Zhong Yicheng slept neither day nor night, nor did he eat or drink much, but he unceasingly urinated and sweated non-stop. Every twenty minutes he urinated. After five days, his weight fell from 136 pounds to 98 pounds; he had cast off his form, changed his appearance. Song Ming saw him looking like this and encouraged him: "Thoroughly remold yourself, thoroughly remold yourself, you've only just started!"

March 1967

The people had organized a meeting to criticize Wei, who was wedged between Zhong Yicheng on the right and Song Ming, who was also being criticized, on the left. Zhong Yicheng was pressed down into "kneeling" position on the platform to show that he was different from Wei and Song Ming. This showed the "policy" of differential treatment.

The Revolutionary Rebel clique said: "Wei ———— is known for his lectures on the Party. He recklessly spewed out poison and wildly attracted attention to Liu Shaoqi's sinister method of 'cultivation.'[7] He propagated the theory that one should behave like a robot, the theory of merging private and public, the theory of suffering small losses for great gains . . . He's a capitalist roader; he consistently covered up for fake Party members and put them in important positions. This true rightist, Zhong Yicheng, consistently covered up for and promoted the anti-revolutionary revisionary theorist Song Ming . . ."

"Smash Wei ———! Overthrow Song Ming! Zhong Yicheng will never change!"

"Crush Wei ———'s dog head! If Song Ming doesn't tell the truth then knock him down!"

"Only the left is allowed to revolt, the right must not be allowed to cause trouble! If Zhong Yicheng wants to reverse this verdict let him taste the iron fist of the proletariat!"

Zhong Yicheng was miserably uneasy, because he knew that when they had searched his house they had confiscated his detailed notes of Wei's lectures on the

7. This refers to a speech by Liu Shaoqi (1900–1969) entitled *The Cultivation of a Communist Party Member (Lun gongchandangyuan de xiuyang)*. The speech was originally given in 1939 at the Institute of Marxism-Leninism in Yan'an. It was printed several times in periodicals, and when Liu was criticized in 1966, the speech was criticized for portraying communism as a matter of self-discipline and self-cultivation rather than class struggle over economic issues.

Party in 1951. In order to lay their hands on these notes, the Revolutionary Rebel clique and the Proletarian Revolutionary clique had cracked open heads and spilt blood. Seven were injured, one severely. Later, when they called this criticism meeting these ever-precious notes of his were used as "negative lessons." Because he was so miserable he unknowingly curled up his body. This made the hand grabbing his hair cruelly tighten its grip. He was pushed down, then up, then down again.

That evening, Song Ming killed himself. For a long time his nerves had been steadily deteriorating, so he had kept a lot of sleeping pills on hand. This event impressed Zhong Yicheng very strongly. He had never believed Song Ming was a bad person. Every day Song Ming read deep into the night: Marx, Lenin, and Mao, Central Committee documents, Party reports and Party publications. He poured his heart into using inference and deduction to analyze people's thinking. He analyzed every little sesame seed into a watermelon, and actually thought he was "helping" people. In '57 he had taken great relish in logically and with surprising ingenuity analyzing, bit by bit, everything that Zhong Yicheng had ever said. He had proved that Zhong Yicheng was a capitalist rightist from head to foot. "It doesn't matter if you are aware of it or not, if you subjectively perceive it or not, your class instinct seeps out. The true essence of your words and actions, the nature of which does not move in obeisance to your subjective will, is anti-Party and anti-socialist," he said. He gave examples: "For example, you like to ask people 'Will it rain today?' There's a sentence in one of your poems. 'Who knows if tomorrow will be clear or cloudy?' What does this mean? This is the typical uneasiness of the declining classes . . ." Song Ming's analysis left Zhong Yicheng tongue-tied and dumbfounded, full of both fear and admiration. But at the same time that he carried out this analysis, Song Ming was still concerned about Zhong Yicheng and helped him in matters of daily life. When it rained, he lent Zhong Yicheng his raincoat, and when they were eating dumplings in the cafeteria he poured out some vinegar for him. After the "treatment" was over, he warmly and sincerely grasped Zhong Yicheng's hand: "You have a future before you, but you must exchange your soul for a new one. I hope you can go forward to the very end on the road of self-transformation, and become a totally new person." On another occasion: "Thoroughly forget about your little self and throw yourself into the fire of revolution!" He said many enthusiastic and sincere things which Zhong Yicheng, in his sorry state, felt were the words of a good friend. But so it goes that Song Ming was weak himself. He had chosen a road he did not really have to take, and when the gusts of the great Cultural Revolution so lightly and softly blew against him, he could not bear it. May he rest in peace.

1979

A gray shadow cut into Zhong Yicheng's bedroom. The gray shadow was wearing a short-sleeved "Teliling" brand shirt and high-quality polyester pants. It had long hair and a filter cigarette dangling from the side of its mouth, and was clutching a Hawaiian electric guitar to its chest. It was a young man. A mini tape recorder was stuffed into his pocket along with several tapes on which he had recorded "precious" Hong Kong tunes. No, he wasn't young, he was nearly fifty. He had dropsy in his upper eyelids, his mouth was a little awry, his teeth, tongue, and hands were all stained brownish-yellow by harsh tobacco. His mouth was filled with the odor of liquor, but his face carried a pleasant smile. Then again maybe he was only a little over forty. He had big eyes and double-folded eyelids, and his entire body from top to bottom was trim and spotless. He took care in eating, dressing, and social intercourse. The look on his face was a total blank, and the expression in his eyes the emptiness of one with no special skills. Or, it could be a woman who had aged early, grayed prematurely and was mumbling and sighing in despair. Or it could be something else again. Altogether, they were one shadow that often came near our dwellings in the seventies.

The gray shadow twisted his tongue around, curled his lips, and said, "It's all a bunch of crap. No matter if it's the training of a Communist Party member or if it's the spirit of the Revolutionary Rebels. No matter if it's surpass England in three years or surpass America in ten, we won't catch up or surpass them in fifty years. No matter if it's the Bolshevik salute or the salute of the Red Guards, and no matter if it's 'adore with all your heart' or 'long live, long live.' No matter if it's a real Communist Party member or if it's a capitalist in the Party. No matter if it's punish others or get punished, and no matter if it's August 18 or April 5.[8] It's crap, it's a bunch of crap, it's stupid . . ."

"Then there's nothing true in the end? In the end there's nothing that affects you, that makes you want to live on?" Zhong Yicheng asked.

"Love, youth, and freedom; other than what I have myself, I believe nothing. Let's drink to friendship! Actually, I saw through things and cut myself loose long ago. In '57 when they wanted me to go to a meeting to air my views, I told them nothing! For twenty

8. August 18, 1966, when Mao Zedong first inspected the Red Guards at Tian'anmen Square, marks the beginning of the Red Guard Movement, in which thousands of high-school and college students traveled over China to set up revolutionary headquarters and carry on the revolution. The April 5, 1976, demonstration in Tian'anmen Square to commemorate the death of Zhou Enlai, who was perceived by many as a moderate who tried to mitigate the leftist policies of the Cultural Revolution, protested the policies of the "Gang of Four," who were arrested in the fall of 1976 after the death of Mao in September. This demonstration marks the end of the Cultural Revolution.

years I haven't read books or newspapers, I've just gone on as usual picking up my paycheck.

"It's just rotten luck to be born Chinese. Anyway things won't get better in China in my lifetime, so let's just forget it and loosen things up . . . My daughter is working on her thirty-fourth boyfriend, but none are satisfactory to me, she can't . . ." the gray shadow said.

"All right, for the moment we won't discuss whether your demands are reasonable or not," Zhong Yicheng said. "I just want to know, for your country, for the people, or even just for yourself, for your love and freedom, for your friends and your liquor, so you can drift along and talk big about loosening things up, and for your daughter . . . no, I should ask what you are planning to do to find an ideal son-in-law? What have you done? What are you prepared to do? What do you have power to do?"

". . . idiot! Pitiful! Up to now you've just been bound by yourself; hasn't your poor fortune woken you up a little?" The gray shadow got angry and turned defence into attack.

"Yes, I've been an idiot before. It's quite possible that our love and admiration contained some stupidity, our loyalty and sincerity some blindness, and our convictions some naiveté. It's quite possible that our demands are not realistic, our enthusiasm not always warranted, and that seeds of deception were buried in our reverence. Our job is more difficult and bothersome than it has ever been before. But in the end we still have love and admiration, loyalty and sincerity, convictions, demands, enthusiasm, reverence, and a job to do. We had them before, and from now on, if we refuse to whine like children, they will turn into stronger and more mature kernels inside us. And when our love, convictions, loyalty, and sincerity are ravaged, we still have anger and pain, and even more we have hopes that can never die. Our lives and souls were bright before and will be brighter from now on. But what about you? My gray friend, what do you have? What have you done? What can you do? What are you except one big nothing?"

V

But I believe in the Party! Our great, glorious, true Party! The Party has wiped dry so many tears and opened up such a future! Without the Party, I would be only a struggling insect on the verge of death. It was the Party that made me into a Communist Party member, a revolutionary cadre, one of those who hold up the heavens and the earth. I understand our Party, because even though I sneaked in, I ended up living in the Party for over ten years. For over ten years I used my unbiased child's eyes to look and examine. I read Party magazines, worked in Party organizations and participated in Party meetings. I came into contact with many Party cadres, including leaders; they liked me, and I loved them. I knew the Party had been put together by an anxious country and a worried people, by the flower of the Chinese race and all the social classes; it was the sad, fervent song and the unselfish creation of a people willing to bear a cross for their liberation. Have you read "Wonderful China" by the war martyr Fang Zhimin? Have you read the poetry Xia Minghan wrote before he went to his execution?[9] We have read them and know they are real. We

9. Xia Minghan (1900–1928), a communist revolutionary who worked among peasants and advocated arming them, was arrested and killed by the Nationalists in 1928. Fang Zhimin (1899–1935),

believe them, because we believe that under those cir-
cumstances we would do what Fang Zhimin and Xia
Minghan did. We know the Party must benefit no one
other than the classes, the race, and the people. It is
precisely because of this that the Party has the right
and the responsibility to make strict demands on each
of its members. Party members also can and must
mercilessly bring forward extremely strict and well-
defined demands on their own part. My early entry
into the Party should not become a reason for compas-
sion, forgiveness, or protection, but rather a basis for
even stricter demands. Furthermore, the Party's criticism of me did not result from any one person's dislike
or any personal motivation. For the Party's cause, for
internationalism, for the death struggle with capital-
ism and revisionism inside and outside the country,
the Party was unselfish and unbending! The Party was
great and strong! Even if I had said and written
things disadvantageous to the Party only unconsciously, even if I had only wavered a second while
dreaming, the Party should still adopt resolute mea-
sures to deal with me. If I should be totally eliminated
from the Party, then kick me out! If I should be labeled a rightist element then label me! If the dictatorship of the proletariat should prevail, then it should
prevail! Shoot those who should be shot! Just like

founder of the Tenth Red Army of Peasants and Workers, was killed
by the Nationalists.

Nagy in Hungary was shot. If it was necessary for China to kill some rightists, if she had to kill me, I would put my head on the chopping block with no regrets! Although I had been called a rightist, I still wanted to live on. The reason I could live on was that my faith was unshakable, as hard as stone and as solid as a mountain!

It was 5:00 P.M. on March 8, 1958, under the stone bridge on the Jinpo River. It was raining lightly. Gusts of wind blew the rain across the faces and clothes of Zhong Yicheng and Ling Xue, and across the still temporarily dry riverbed on which they were standing. The winter air cut into their cold bones; hardly anyone was out. Ever since Zhong Yicheng had been criticized he had stayed hidden from Ling Xue, and then she had been sent out for several months on a job outside the province, so they had not seen each other for a long time. He had set up this meeting because he planned to have a final talk with Ling Xue. The worst time was already past; it had been painful to deny and destroy himself, but nonetheless, his basic faith had given him the strength to go through this unthinkable and unspeakable difficulty and pain. His faith in the Party had not wavered or weakened in the slightest, but rather, his inexpressible love and great respect had increased as he was being purged. So, in the chilly wind and sharp rain of a spring day's twilight, under the Jinpo River stone bridge, where the scenery was the same as in ancient times (actually, other than the

bridge itself, the surrounding scenery had changed—
many new buildings had gone up), although the young
Communist Party member who had bravely defended
this stone bridge before had now turned into an "element," although his insides had been cut out and his
heart shredded by knives, the Party that had liberated this stone bridge and this city still existed. It existed not only in the municipal and district commit-
tees, but also in the factories and villages. Moreover,
it had an honored, solid, and glorious existence in
Zhong Yicheng's heart, and although a surgical knife
had scooped out his own heart, it could not dig out this
brilliant image of the Party. So what he had to say to
Ling Xue was of course upright, awe-inspiring, and
earth-shattering:

"I don't think I ever knew how bad I really was!
From childhood on my soul was full of the poisonous
germs of individualism and heroism. When I was a
student I always wanted to be tops in my schoolwork,
ahead of everyone else. My motives for entering the
Party were impure; I hoped I could do some great
deed and go down as an important personage in the
annals of history! And I held to absolute egalitarian-
ism regardless of work, to liberalism and sentimentalism . . . At the critical moment of socialist revolution,
all these ideas became the irreconcilable opponents of
the Party and socialism. They made me into the Party's internal enemy! Don't say anything, Ling Xue,
just listen to me. For example, the comrades criticized

me because, they said, I had a profound hatred of the
Party system. At first I didn't think so, but they told
me if I didn't think so to think harder, put a little effort
into it and I'd finally see. Later I thought of the time
two months ago we went to eat in that Cantonese restaurant next to the Xinhua Bookstore and waited for
an hour for the food, but they had forgotten to make
it . . . Then I got angry, do you still remember? At the
time you told me to take it easy, but I said, 'This kind
of sloppy work is worse than it was under private
ownership!' You see? What kind of talk is that? Isn't
it dissatisfaction with socialism? I confessed this sentence and was criticized for it . . . Ah, Ling Xue, don't
shake your head, no matter what, you shouldn't disbe-
lieve or doubt me, and certainly don't be dissatisfied
with the Party. Even the tiniest dissatisfaction will
sprout like a seed in your heart, grow roots, get big,
and eventually take off in the evil direction of opposition to the Party. I'm bad, I'm an enemy; I was impure
to start with and later got worse. You should throw
me out without the slightest hesitation, draw a bound-
ary between us, despise me! I've betrayed your love
and befouled your Bolshevik salute! Just as I was
thrown out of the Party, let me be forever thrown out
of your heart!"

Zhong Yicheng could not go on. A bitter, sharp gas
that burned like fire smoldered in his throat. His voice
became mute, and tears came pouring out and ran
down his face. He quickly turned around. He origi-

nally had not planned to show any sadness or pain. During the days he was being criticized, he had thought of Ling Xue so many times; he had thought of each street they had walked together, each meal they had eaten together, each movie frame they had seen together, and each song they had sung and softly hummed together. Their love had been built on mutual Bolshevik salutes and mutual exchange of advice. He had written a love poem that was later mocked and misunderstood, but he had written it honestly and with deep feeling. The title of the love poem was "Give Me Some Advice." It went like this:

> Give me some advice,
> Make me more perfect and pure,
> Give me some advice,
> Make me more earnest and true.
>
> We have no youth, we
> Have given our youth to the storm.
> We model ourselves after the brave sea bird
> That spreads its wings and flies into thunder
>   and lightening.
>
> We have no self, we
> Have given ourselves to the revolution.
> We model ourselves on past martyrs. Liu
>   Hulan and Zoya sadden yet inspire.[10]

10. Liu Hulan and Zoya were Chinese and Russian female revolutionaries who died young. Liu Hulan died at age fifteen.

For the national anthem, the hammer and
  sickle,
For the loyalty and sincerity of a Communist
  Party member,
For the heavy burdens and long road of our
  cause,
Give me some advice, please criticize me!

In the deep, deep black night,
Advice is a light.
In the vast, vast sky,
Advice is a star.
In the parched land,
Advice is the rain.
To the sailboat waiting to sail.
Advice is the wind.

In my heart, my dear comrade,
Your advice is my love, my love!

What a warm love poem! Let those of the future
mock it, doubt it, and scorn it. Let them claim that we
didn't understand poetry, human feelings, that we
were doctrinaire and "leftist." However, after he became an "element," reading over this poem was still a
good, beautiful, rich, and warm experience for Zhong
Yicheng.

But now none of this belonged to him anymore. All
of it was done with; the foundation had been dug out
and discarded, the fire taken out from under the pot.
The mutual Bolshevik salute was impossible, and
there was nowhere to start with comradely advice. He

had decided the only thing to do was to end their contact without a moment's pause—firmly, thoroughly, and with no delay. He had to act with total resolution or Ling Xue would not agree. Any show of hurt would just make Ling Xue love him more dearly and make her miserable, and her willingness to part would be only feigned. The result would be that his ugly form would sully and pollute the pure and flawless Ling Xue—that would be a huge, unpardonable sin. So he absolutely must not cry. He firmly had believed he would not cry, because all his tears had already been cried out. His reactionary thinking and anti-Party sins had already proven that he was totally heartless. But what he had imagined was at odds with reality. In his imagination the break-up had been completely logical and without difficulties, easily accomplished in a few words. But this afternoon, when he saw Ling Xue's familiar face, her familiar soft, black hair with its aroma of soap, her shiny, proud, dignified nose, her simple, elegant clothes, when he heard her clear, calm, attractive voice, when he felt her warmth and breath, and when he had finished verbalizing the mental notes that had brewed so long inside him, he cried. He cried wildly, and the chilly wind and bitter rain turned darker and more dismal. Bolshevik salute, Bolshevik salute, Bolshevik salute, Bolshevik salute, it seemed as if this chorus and call still echoed in the faraway edges of the sky, and still refracted in the rainbow hues and rays of evening sunlight. And he truly had sunk, sunk, sunk to the lowest depths, sunk to the blackest void. He opened his mouth. Tears and rain, salty and bitter water flowed into him together.

"No, no, don't talk like that, don't talk like that!" Ling Xue walked around Zhong Yicheng in a panic, searching for his evasive eyes. She grasped his hand without a thought, stroked his hair and face, and pulled his chin up to face her. "What's wrong with you? What's wrong with you? If you've done something wrong, then you criticize yourself, you fix it, so what's the big deal? Why do you have to say so many irrelevant things? I don't understand how things could have been like that. I'm all mixed up, I don't believe it, I can't believe you're any enemy. I only believe those things that actually exist, the actual things you can believe, I don't believe the analysis of them. Don't exaggerate, don't be swayed by your emotions, don't make things bigger than they are, and don't believe everything you hear. The criticism of 'Little Winter Wheat Tells Its Tale' was absurd! They're wrong to label you a rightist, they're mistaken. What's so great about what other people have to say about you—don't you yourself know what you are? Maybe you don't, but I have faith in you! If even you don't have faith, if even you yourself don't have faith, how can we have faith? How can we go on living? As for the rest, I don't know, I don't understand. It's not just that we don't know things outside our galaxy, or things 200,000 years in the past or future; there are some things we still don't know and understand even in our own lives, in the life of our Party. If we don't know, we don't know. If we don't understand, we don't understand. But it can't always be like this, so serious. You have to think about this seriously, but this is so crazy there's no way to think about it seriously. Forgive me, Zhong, in the past you didn't like to hear this, but it's true; you're too young, just too young. I mean you're too little, you're too innocent and enthusiastic, you love dreams too much and you love analysis too much. If you want to talk about what things don't help the cause of the Party, it's precisely these things and nothing else. You think too much and too deeply; how could things have been like that? How can you say black is white and good people are bad? Let them say what they will—you're still Zhong Yicheng! You're the Party's, you're mine, and I'm yours . . . Let's—let's get married! We've been together six or seven years, let's be together forever; if we must endure pain let's endure pain together. Let's go together to try and understand those things we don't understand . . . Maybe it's all just a misunderstanding, a temporary fury. The Party is our dear mother. Dear mothers sometimes will beat their children but children never hold grudges against their mothers. When she's done her anger goes away and the child has a cry upstairs. Maybe this is just a special educational method to build up your vigilance and keep you on your feet. It gives you a big shove and then you can make yourself even better . . . Maybe there'll be a new investigation this month, they'll reconsider your affair and decide they went too far during the movement. You can't correct something until it's gone too far. When they've corrected things, everything will go back to its normal workings . . . It's all right, it's all right, let's . . . together seven or eight years, you're too hard on yourself . . ."

Her words, her voice, and her loving concern produced a marvelous strength in Zhong Yicheng, and he felt soothed and calmed. The world was still the beautiful place it had always been, the Jinpo River bridge was still the durable old bridge of before, and people were still pure and sincere. His language, which had been poisoned and sullied, his attitude made imperious and coarse, his imposing manner, warped by a mountainous pressure, his frozen heart and soul had started to melt and come back to life under her kind and trusting face. Her love radiated like the sun on a spring day. "Bolshevik salute, Bolshevik salute, Bolshevik salute!" This chorus and call, these rays of evening sunlight and rainbow hues once again became the call of his strangled soul and the support of his tottering heart. Because there was Ling Xue, there would be no misery in the world. Because there was Ling Xue, there would be no treachery, no maligning, no humiliation. He buried his head in Ling Xue's bosom, forgetting everything, immersing himself in this love—one imperiled and insulted, but still flawless and complete.

1951–58

We are a generation of light; we have a love full of light. No one can take away the light in our hearts; no one can take away the love in our hearts. When we were young children, we struggled in the darkness. When we got a little older, we moved from the darkness toward light. The night was too black, too dark, so we saw the morning as a flash of light, endless radiance. We shouted and leapt, running toward the light, embracing the light, not aware of the shadows there too. We thought the shadows had died with the black night; we thought the sun above our heads would forever be a morning sun.

Therefore we loved. We loved the Party, loved the red flag, loved "The Internationale," loved Chairman Mao, loved Stalin, and loved Kim Il-Sung, Ho Chiminh, Gheorghiv-Dej, Pieck, and all the Communist Parties of the world, all the leaders of the workers' parties; we loved each Party member, each leader, each branch secretary, and each group leader.[11] We

11. Gheorghe Gheorghiu-Dej (1901–65) was a Rumanian communist leader. Wilhelm Pieck (1876–1960) was East German presi-

loved each laborer and everything each of them created; we loved the newly built department store and theater, the tractors and combines fresh from the factory, the newly installed traffic and street lights, the newly built roads and buildings. We loved the red kerchiefs on the children's breasts, loved the laughter and songs of children who walked arm in arm, loved the tender sprouts on the willow tree, loved the squishy sound of stepping on new winter snow, loved the water, loved the wind, loved the little wheat and the wild chrysanthemums, and loved the fields of good harvest. All of this belonged to the Party, to the people's government, to our new life, and to us.

Love made the light even more brilliant, and the light turned our love into a deeper, stronger love.

So from the night we heard Wei lecture on the training of a Communist Party member, we loved each other. After the lecture, we didn't take the bus; we thought we would walk a ways to the next stop and then get on, but we ended up walking halfway across the city. We walked under the street lamps, our shadows sometimes long, sometimes short, sometimes in front, sometimes in back. The rhythm of our hearts also rose and fell. When we had walked for a long time, we shrunk with cold from the night wind, but our hearts had turned warmer. "Can Bolshevism be

dent from 1949 to 1960. Ho Chi-minh (1890–1969) was Vietnamese Labor Party Chairman.

realized in ten years?" "If ten years isn't enough, then fifteen years." "How can we obliterate individualism faster and more completely?" "We'll always do what the Party says, and be good Party members." "But why was I so irritable with ——— that day; 'comrade' is such a precious title, but I . . ." "I want to take Wei as my goal, I want to be just as simple and mature as him, and just as patient . . . When will I ever be like him?" "You can, you can, I'm sure you can!" "Is it possible that we could think of anything other than being real, qualified Party members and performing our duty to the Party even better? We're ready to lay down our lives for the Party, how could it be that we're unwilling to give up our own shortcomings?" "Yes, yes, I'm just afraid I won't see them, won't perceive them. If I recognize them, I'm sure I will change. I won't give myself the slightest leeway. If you recognize something as a shortcoming but are unwilling to change it, what kind of a Party member are you anyway?" "But changing yourself can't be taken lightly, you need your own subjective effort and the supervision of the people." "Then you supervise first and give me some advice . . ." "My advice . . ." "Ah, you're so right, you're so right, your ideas are perfect; I'll do just as you say. Now, I'll give you some . . ."

Give me some advice—this is love. Ridiculous? Doctrinaire? But isn't one of the reasons love is so precious exactly that it has the power to make people and life more beautiful, strong, and complete? It is a primary force that starts in the heart, and chases the rays of light, races toward the light. Why are the willow twigs so thick and dense and so gentle and soft? Why is the cassia tree so heavy and solid and so dark and deep? Why is the parasol tree so modest and friendly and so graceful and poised? Why is the sky so blue, the flag so red, the light so bright? Why did you and I and he all show smiling faces of happiness and pride? To make the world more good and beautiful, it is necessary first to make each person more good and beautiful. To make oneself more able to love and worthy of being loved, one must first make oneself more lovable. To be able to understand our cause and struggle and life's true significance, we must first brighten our souls a little. So we went after each other's advice as though we were dying of thirst and hunger, and we encouraged each other to conquer our respective shortcomings. It got to the point where in place of "kisses" in our letters, we would write "Bolshevik salute!" Were we behaving like children? An immature sickness of the "left"? Something people later would see as entirely unwarranted? Since we were brought up on the milk of the Party, since the iron convictions of the Party dominated our minds, the hot blood flowing in our bodies was ready at all times to pour out for the Party, our eyes were attentive for the Party, our ears listened carefully for the Party, and our hearts beat for the Party. Since Comrade Stalin had said the Communist Party was made of special stuff, since we were putting all our effort into being, both in name and substance, Party members made of special stuff, and since without the Party neither you nor I would exist, our lives would not exist, we would not have been able to meet in this life nor would we have such unconditional faith in each other (our ancestors and descendants should always envy us this meeting and this mutual faith!), how could we not ask each other questions in the same way the Party did, how could we not be proud, happy, and more deeply in love because of this special way of asking questions?

Often we could not see each other because of Party work or responsibilities, or we would make a date but be unable to keep it. One time one of us was waiting for the other at the door of the theater. I won't say if it was Zhong Yicheng or Ling Xue, because we each had experiences of this kind. This time one of us was responsible for suppressing the Yiguan Dao Society, and so could not be there on time.[12] It was too late to call. Finally this person made it to the theater after an hour and a half. The other was waiting there calmly, not at all upset. "I'm sorry, I'm sorry," the second person said in agitation. "What's there to be sorry about? You didn't come, so I knew you were busy, had responsibilities. I stood here waiting for you while you

12. Yiguan Dao, a secret religious group that demanded allegiance from its members, was suppressed by the Communist Party as feudal and superstitious.

were busy over there; you didn't make a mess of your work just because I was waiting for you—that's the way it should be!" When the movie was over they walked along with the people who had seen the movie, but to others they looked more satisfied and happier than those who had enjoyed and understood the movie the best.

And there was one time when one person waited for the other for seven hours. That person used the seven hours to read over several of Chairman Mao's articles. In seven hours the sky went from light through twilight to black. Afternoon had already changed into evening and the sun had already become stars. Each rustle of sound and movement made this person think the other was coming, every tiny sound seemed like the sound of this lover's far-away footsteps coming close. This person was worried, and picked up the Party Constitution and studied: "The Chinese Communist Party is the vanguard unit of the Chinese workers' class. . . . It has organized armed forces. . . . a high-level form organized by class. . . ." Only the next day did this person find out that right at their meeting time the other person had received a notice to go to the Municipal Committee for a meeting because Chairman Mao was coming to inspect the work here. This news, coming the day after an anxious yet quiet wait of seven hours, was cause for great joy . . .

We had walked every street of the city together and

had gone through every year since liberation together. We were endlessly amazed that we were able
to live so happily in this great Party. With the Party's
introduction, we discovered each other quickly and
without any doubt or hesitation. We knew nothing of
sizing up qualifications, making demands on each
other, or having reservations. It seemed as if our love
was preordained from birth. We never thought our
lives could be otherwise.

Human beings invented language and used it to con-
vey, describe, and record good and beautiful things
and make them even better. But there are some
people who schemingly use language—coarse and
explosive, arbitrary and assertive, murderous—to
break down this goodness and beauty and destroy
every good and beautiful heart. Some people have had
great success in this area. But they didn't succeed
completely; a bit of light and love remained indestruc-
tibly buried in our hearts and steeped in our blood-
streams. We were the generation of light, and our love
was bright. No one could steal the light in our hearts;
no one could steal the love in our hearts.

April 1958

It was May Day eve, a fresh, beautiful moment.
The sun's rays, which had gone through the withering
sag of the winter season, once again became radiant

and beautiful. The soft branches and twigs and the newly green leaves flourished more with every day, and already blocked the sky on both sides of the street. They were spotless, fresh, and lively as if they had sprouted just yesterday. Everywhere under the trees girls were selling strawberries; tender, red, juicy, sweet with a touch of bitterness, the strawberries carried the fresh smell of green grass that beguiled you, just as the times and the lively city did. People were changing their clothing. The old-fashioned elderly had not yet taken off their big-toed padded shoes, and the weak and sick were still wrapped up in thick wool scarves, but the young had already put on their brightly colored sweaters or even their thin white shirts to call out for summer and for life. It was on this kind of a bright, clear day, in a green spring, that Zhong Yicheng and Ling Xue got married.

Their world was bright, their struggle was great, and their lives were good and beautiful. Zhong Yicheng firmly and absolutely believed this; people could stand up under anything they had created themselves. There was such a thing as a happiness people could not endure, but there was no unbearable pain. In his childhood, his father's poor friends had liked to encourage and comfort each other with these tame words. Yes, indeed, there had been criticism, struggle, the label of an "element," propaganda describing him as a "deadly enemy," exposure of his "ugly visage," expulsion from the Party; he had gone through these things one after another. Pain was hard to endure, but it would not kill you. Ling Xue had been right, the important thing was your own confidence in yourself. If you yourself did not collapse, no one had any way to break you through punishment, even if they punished you to death. Maybe he actually had made some terrible mistakes—or call them "crimes," but maybe his errors were not so serious. Maybe he had been criticized and dragged down as "stinking," but maybe in reality he was not so stinking after all. He was still unable to tell clearly himself. But one thing was certain—he wanted to live on, to be in the revolution, to change his thinking and to be a true communist soldier. He could do this because he wanted to so fiercely, more fiercely than he wanted anything else.

So he recovered his health, his enthusiasm, and his optimistic view of life. During the first month of wedding preparations, he and Ling Xue had many pictures taken together. The decision on a method of dealing with him was "pending," so he didn't have to participate in a lot of meetings. He had lots of time for love and never missed any dates. He always went on time and felt himself fortunate to be able to spend so much time with Ling Xue. One picture was taken like this: He was hot from mountain climbing, so he took off the shirt of his uniform. With one hand he clasped the shirt, which was thrown over his shoulder. His

other hand was on his hips. The evening sun was shining on his face and the clear wind was blowing his hair;
the background was the crisscross of paths in the
fields beneath the mountains. When this picture was
printed it astonished and even shocked Zhong Yicheng. In his terrible state, how could his picture be
so spirited, carefree, confident, vigorous, and full of
joy?

He should be like that. He was like that originally.
He was the sea bird that fought the storm; he was the
eagle that soared in the sky. He was a spring flower
bathing delightedly in the rays of the sun. No matter
what elaborate technique he used to compose his
expression, his face could not assume the expression
of fear mixed with emptiness and fawning mixed with
awe characteristic of those labeled landlords, rich
peasants, anti-revolutionaries, bad elements, rightists. He had no way to be a rightist as he was supposed to be, and he felt bad about this.

But he didn't dare show the pictures to anyone else,
nor let people know that he went to have his picture
taken with Ling Xue every Sunday. He had to
sneak around and be a just and honorable person in
secret . . .

. . . That evening they got married. Other than a
few close relatives, they had invited no one. Even
among the close relatives, there were several who
gave excuses not to come. Also, this very morning a
leader at Ling Xue's factory (after junior high school

Ling Xue had gone to a technical high school and was now a technician in a factory) had tried to "rescue" her for the last time. Because she stubbornly refused to draw a clear line between herself and Zhong Yicheng, she could not take a firm stand in struggling against and exposing him; now, when the crown of blame had been placed firmly on Zhong Yicheng's head, and it was still new enough to cause pain to look at it, she had petitioned five times in one month to marry him. Ling Xue refused her last rescue, so this afternoon the branch had called a meeting and expelled her from the Party.

Ling Xue didn't accept this punishment. When the vote was taken she didn't raise her hand. When asked to write her opinion, she wrote the word "none" without any agitation. Because of this she received a warning: "unprincipled attitude" and "don't let it get worse."

Two hours later, she changed into a purple and green shirt, a yellow sweater, a pair of gray serge trousers, and low-heeled black leather shoes; she got on the bus and went to "marry herself off."

It was a totally desolate, or rather, frighteningly desolate marriage ceremony. Other than their two mothers (neither of them had fathers), their younger sisters and brothers, and two neighbors who did odd jobs on the street, no one was there. A plate of salted watermelon seeds, a plate of fruit drops, a plate of candied fruit, and a few cups of tea were the only refreshments. Ling Xue told Zhong Yicheng what had happened that morning and afternoon. She did not feel this was an attack on their union at all; rather, it seemed to increase its significance. When the sky and earth were collapsing, they linked their arms together. For a second Zhong Yicheng's face paled and his eyebrows knit together; he had gone through a lot himself, but an attack on Ling Xue made him feel worse then one on himself. But the corners of Ling Xue's stubborn mouth showed a smile, no sadness or pain, and from her eyes flowed an overwhelming tenderness, but no anger or blame. In each of her movements was delight and total happiness, not loneliness or sorrow. So Zhong Yicheng smiled too. For seven years they had been together, yet not together—it had been so hard! Now they would be together forever; he thanked fate, thanked Ling Xue's true feeling for him, thanked the sun, the moon, the earth, and every star.

By 9:00 P.M. there was no one left in that room. But there was still a radio broadcasting fervent tunes. Ling Xue turned off the radio and said, "Let's sing together. Let's sing from start to finish all the songs we loved to sing when we were children. You know, I've never kept a diary. The way I remember things is through songs—each song represents a year, and as soon as I sing it I think of the things I want to remember." "Me too, me too," Zhong Yicheng said. "Which year shall we start with?" "Forty-six." "What did you

sing in '46?" "I sang 'Kaqiusha.' I learned it in '46."
"OK, after we sing that one, let's sing 'Brothers, On
toward the Sun, toward Freedom.' What about '47?"
"In '47 I loved to sing this song the best; this was the
song I loved to sing when I entered the Party . . .

> We are the ones who cleared the way,
> We are the ones who chopped the trees.
> With our own hands we built
> The house that reached the sky.

"Then on each road I walked I sang this song, and I
felt that all of the old world was under my feet. . . ."
"Forty-eight, in '48 I sang 'The sky will soon be light,
it's such a black night, it's such a hard way, people fall
every day' . . ." "Forty-nine?" "There are too many
songs for '49. 'Without the Communist Party There
Would Be No China,' 'When the Great Flag Is Raised
the Whole Sky Is Red.' In '50, 'The Five-Starred Red
Flag Flutters in the Wind,' 'We'll Run a Race with
Time'; in '51, 'Gallantly and Vigorously,' 'Long White
Mountain Range . . .' Remember, we all wanted to go
to Korea then . . ." They started to sing, and the clear
tones of their songs, full of moving light and the happiness of spring, made up for everything they had
been deprived of. This was how they recalled the
months and years of purity and intensity, encouraging
and comforting each other's hearts, wounded but still
brightly burning.

They sang so happily that they did not hear the

knock on the door or the sound of the door opening. When they heard someone call "Zhong" and "Ling" and heard the sound of footsteps, they turned around and looked—it was just as if guests had dropped down from the sky. Three people—District Committee Secretary Wei, his ailing wife, and his chauffeur, Gao.

During the movement Wei had got thinner too; his lower eyelids looked as if they had a bit of dropsy, and the lines in the corners of his mouth were even more obvious. Wei's wife, originally from the country, was a cadre in the women's movement. She was very dark and very thin. During the process of "criticism and struggle" against Zhong Yicheng, she had never said a word, but just looked at him with perplexed, sympathetic, and comforting eyes. Zhong Yicheng could not forget this. In those days of struggle, any people who poured out a glass of water for him, nodded to him, smiled at him, or used even slightly restrained words when they talked about him were all firmly lodged in his heart. He would be moved by the thought of them all his life. Wei and his wife had appeared with friendly and affable faces, but the chauffeur, just a youngster, stood impatiently tapping one foot and making clucking noises.

"You rascal you, you managed to keep the news from me." Wei's strong voice, his concerned and kind attitude made Zhong Yicheng think of his feelings at the scene of the first meeting of Party members in '49 when Wei had given him his overcoat. Wei waved him

toward the presents his wife had brought out: a set of
embroidered pillows, a photo album, and two beauti-
fully and artistically made diaries. "Bring out the wine
and let us drink to the happiness of you both . . ." he
shouted.

"But, but . . ." Zhong Yicheng turned awkward and
appeared to be at a loss. "We don't have any wine."
We spoke in a small, quivering voice.

"What, what?" Wei did not seem to understand
what he had said. "Why don't you have any wine? This
is the wine of good cheer, we've come to drink your
wine of celebration!"

"If there isn't any let's forget it, the day is almost
over," Wei's wife said warmly.

"I don't want any." The chauffeur let out a snort.

"But I want to drink; I absolutely have to drink
your wine of celebration." Wei seemed to be having a
fit. "Why isn't there any wine? Why isn't there any
wine?" he shouted, his voice full of sorrow and his
eyes moist. Zhong Yicheng, Ling Xue, Wei's wife, and
even the chauffeur could not help but be touched.

"Gao, you go buy some wine!" He looked at his
watch, and with a resolute attitude that permitted no
argument, spoke as though he were giving orders during war. "Complete your mission in half an hour. Since
they won't treat us to wine, we'll get some and drink
to them ourselves—that'll really show them!" He got
up laughing.

From the secretary's look, Gao could tell that he had

better live up to his responsibilities, so he left in a hurry. After twenty minutes Gao came back panting. "No luck, the store closed a long time ago, and the all-night stand by the train station has to do the accounts from last month, so they've closed for a day," he said. "Don't we have any wine at home?" Wei asked in disbelief and with a strange fury. "No," his wife said apologetically, as if it were her fault that they couldn't drink any wine. "You don't drink. And the doctor won't let you drink . . . Oh yes, we have a bottle of cooking wine that's used in food preparation." "Can you drink cooking wine? Of course, if you wanted to drink it you could," Wei asked and answered himself, then gave an order. "Give the house key to Gao so he can go and get that cooking wine!"

After Gao left, Wei talked about this and that, but he did not talk about what had just happened, and he did not talk about the sadness that had welled up in him. In a second, Zhong Yicheng also forgot about those utterly preposterous things. From the moment Wei had arrived, he had seemed to have something to rely on, some pillar of confidence. It was like being in the middle of a nightmare and hearing the call of someone who was awake—as soon as you moved, opened your eyes, all of the terror and confusion would disappear into the darkness . . .

Gao came back, but what he brought with him was not cooking wine. It was an unopened bottle of Mao Tai—he had brought out his own home's "reserves."

"To Comrade Zhong Yicheng and Comrade Ling Xue's new marriage, to their happiness, to their certain conquering of problems on the road ahead, to . . . in the end . . . bottoms up!"

Wei raised his glass with dignity. Zhong Yicheng and Ling Xue raised theirs, and they drank down this "wine of celebration" that warmed them to the bottom of their hearts. Half of the glass was wine and the other half hot tears.

VI

The train took off flying on a winter's day into an open country that stretched as far as the eye could see. The pale blue haze lifted, nothing blocked the view, and the world looked vast and endless. No snow had piled up yet in this early winter; the stubble from fall harvest and the winter wheat, slightly curled up from the cold but still retaining some green, were clearly visible in the fields. Little winter wheat, "full of harvest's seeds," had only given birth to misery. An improbable coincidence? Or was it a special method of the Party to teach its sons and daughters, to test them through trials? No matter what else, to be a loyal soldier in the Party one had to respond to all of this positively. Wei had shown up for his wedding. Lots of people still treated him normally and with friendship. "Draw the lines clearly" was just something that had happened temporarily under pressure; when the pressure was off a little, the "lines" were not so severe. And then there was Ling Xue, so concerned and crazy about him; she was ten times more attentive and warm toward his wounded heart than she used to be.

Other "rightist elements" had long since gone to the country to undergo "reform through labor" (Zhong Yicheng did not like to say "reform through labor" because those three words made him think of prisoners),

85

but Wei had told Zhong Yicheng to wait. He had heard his problems were going to be reinvestigated. This gave him so much hope that he dared not think about his kind of happiness, just as he had not dared think about this kind of catastrophe. He dreamt that the organization's Branch Secretary came to talk to him. He told him his punishment had been changed to two years of probation in the Party. Even though it was still a harsh punishment, he was so moved that he cried himself awake, and his pillow cover had a big wet patch on it. For half a year he had been filled with hope every morning, and each evening had longed for tomorrow. Tomorrow the black clouds would disperse and everything would be all right; tomorrow all of his grievances and misery would change into a wide and gratified smile. But finally he was informed: "The results of this movement will not be reinvestigated." It was really odd. All of the movements had been reinvestigated—the "tigers" beaten down during the "Three-Anti's" and the "Five-Anti's" had already been cleared through reinvestigation, but this movement alone was not going to be reinvestigated.[13] "What's done is done, and I hope you work hard from now on;

13. The "Three-Anti Movement," a nationwide campaign beginning in August 1951, was directed against cadres and protested corruption, waste, and bureaucracy. The "Five-Anti Movement" was a campaign initiated in January 1952 in industry and commerce against bribery, tax evasion, theft of state property, abuse of state economic information, and cheating on government contracts.

as long as you put effort into reforming your thinking, the day will eventually come when you return to the Party ranks." Right before he left for the country, Wei said these words to him in the office, and they brought him great warmth.

Now he was sitting in the train. Ling Xue's face, with a forced smile as she saw him off at the station, still floated before his eyes. "Bon voyage!" Ling Xue had shouted in a trembling voice as the train started to go. This trembling sound made Zhong Yicheng feel horribly sad. "Ling Xue, I'm sorry, I'm sorry!" he wanted to cry . . .

The steam whistle blew a long note, the wheels clanked, the locomotive heaved deeply, and the smokestack spewed out a thick smoke. When the train went over a bridge it shook violently and when it went through a tunnel the cars were all black (the attendants had forgotten to turn on the lights). The loudspeakers in the cars resounded with the forceful words of the Great Leap Forward and the magnificent tune "Surpass England and Catch Up with America." Each car was competing for red flags. Besides constantly sweeping and bringing water, the attendants also had to sing, read reports, and propagate politics—they had to use their voices and the loudspeakers to compete. All of this beat on Zhong Yicheng's heart like a drumstick and made him momentarily put aside his regret at leaving Ling Xue and the city. Let bygones forever be bygones, life was still strong, fascinating, and fiery. He was only twenty-six, with time and the future before him; he would go forward single-mindedly, he mumbled to himself. Actually he had said these things to himself many times long before he got on the train, but it was only now in the confused noises and varying brightness and darkness of the train, as he sat a ways from the window and greedily watched the fields, roads, ponds, and houses swirl and sweep by, that he truly felt both pain and excitement and happily perceived: "What's done is done, a new life is beginning!"

He was still young, strong, and healthy; he was still in possession of four good limbs and a good head, and he had all of his revolutionary life still in front of him. He was like a flower bud or newly opened flower that had suddenly been hit by a devastating storm. But the nature of flowers is to be fragrant and full of color. Their original inclination is to open, especially if they have good roots, stamens, and pistils, if they have a natural affinity with and affection for the sun, earth, air, and water. Then, if you burn them with fire, poison them with smoke, chop them with knives, or scald them with boiling water, they will still retain a little living root and bud. They live on, taking in the sun's rays and the raindrops, soaking up the earth's nourishment, and once again putting forth branches and sprouting green leaves. Look, in spite of the dense and early lines in the corners of his mouth that gave people a feeling of terror and anguish and got even more obvious when he grinned, his eyes were still bright and optimistic, his nose firm and strong, and his head held high. As the train moved forward and the "drumstick" beat on, fiery, brilliant sparks flew out of his eyes.

After going through one tunnel after another and one patch of blue sky after another, the train reached the station. It stopped at a strategically situated place hemmed in by mountains on three sides and bordered by a large river on another.

Zhong Yicheng looked like a cavalry soldier, carrying his bag on his back and clambering up a rugged mountain road with the help of a thick branch just broken off a tree. Hawks circled above his head, pine and walnut trees stood on the mountain slope, green rocks crouched forbiddingly by the roadside, and water leapt violently through the mountain valleys. Zhong Yicheng did not know where his great energy came from, but he fairly flew as he walked on and on. Because he had waited for a reinvestigation but in the end went to the country as an "element," no one walked with him. But he felt that a giant burst of strength was urging him, driving him on. He couldn't stop, he had to whip himself to go faster on the road of reform. The nation was leaping forward; in another three years the "three discrepancies" would be gone, and they would have begun with communism.[14] Then

14. The "Three Discrepancies" are the discrepancies between

China would become the most flourishing, rich, and progressive nation in the world, with big, totally collective communes—how could she still be mired in the muddy pit of "capitalist classes?" When they reached the point when communism was working all over the country, wouldn't that "capitalist class" be just too comical, inappropriate, and unsightly? He wasn't depressed or afraid. Look, he could go on for three or five hours on a mountain road in one breath. He was dripping with sweat, but the sweat was washing away his shame. Sweating was just the prelude. Youth was a priceless treasure and a never-ending strength, a time when one feared nothing. Even if he had lived wrongly or in vain for twenty-six years, it was a sin of the past, and what was so important about it? From now on didn't he have fifty years left to live once again, be a revolutionary once again; didn't he once again have a chance to be a communist soldier? In fifty years couldn't he do lots and lots of things that would be good for the Party and good for the people? Wasn't fifty years quite long enough for him to remake himself into a useful person? If he were purged and had no way to fulfill his responsibilities to the Party, then let him, for example, study architecture or mathematics; he really used to like mathematics classes, and it was only because of the needs of Party work that he

---

white-collar and blue-collar labor, the city and the country, and workers and peasants.

had turned his energies elsewhere. But no, first he had to reform, to gain qualifications as a citizen and as a person. So he came to the mountains to donate his youth and spend his enthusiasm there as well.

His body was drowning in sweat; even his eyes were having difficulties. Thistles and stickers clung all over the bottom of his trousers. Bits of dust, red, yellow, black, and white, covered the tops of his shoes. Zhong Yicheng climbed past the amber and white mountain where *maya* stone was quarried, climbed past the walnuts, dates, peaches, pears, and almonds, persimmons, and hawthorns covering the slope of a flowered and fruited mountain; only one fiery orange-red persimmon was still hanging on the branch. And when he went by coal mountains as black as ink, where bare-chested mine workers wearing only thin trousers pushed little mine carts out from the stark pit hole, Zhong Yicheng felt extraordinarily close to them. And he walked by gray-yellow mountains of lime, and of course blue-green pines. He ended up at the highest point—Goosewing Peak.

A cool wind blew gently, hot sweat drenched his body; the view abruptly opened up and he could see hundreds of mountains and peaks under his feet. The big river was like a line of silver, twisting and curling right before his eyes. On the flatlands far away, mist wafted, thick and indistinct, and trees and villages were faintly visible, as if they were ships appearing and then disappearing on the sea. The area below his

feet was full of dwellings with black smoke rising from
them, fields crisscrossed with paths, and the tents and
lean-tos of the road crew just then working on construction. Looking back on the road he had come on,
he saw that his several hours of bumpy walking had
thrown not only the city but also the flatlands behind
him. Looking down before him on the vivid mountains
and river and the remote sky and earth, he suddenly
loosened up and felt carefree and happy. He looked at
the four sides around him and was taken by a moment
of surprise; why were this scenery and topography,
tall mountains, flowers, trees and fields, villages and
worksites all so familiar? It was as if he knew them,
as if he somehow had been here and seen this before.
Clearly this was the first time he had come here in his
life, not only to Goosewing Peak, but also the first
time he had been to the mountains or the country.
Why did this scene make him feel so unexpectedly familiar and close to it, as if they were kindred spirits?
Could it be that he had seen a description like this in
some novel? Was it possible that he had seen scenes
like these in some movie? Could he have come here
before in a dream? Was it possible that for so many
years what he had been searching, hoping, and looking for was just exactly this wide earth and sky where
the Party had put him?

I've come, I've been reborn, the past is gone forever, and my new course of development begins here;
he wanted to cry out, sing loudly, whistle, but then he

remembered he could conquer this petty-bourgeois fanaticism. Overly extreme fervor would just bring catastrophe . . . He thought of Ling Xue's advice to him as he was leaving: "Forgive my saying this, but don't be so excitable. We still don't understand lots of things; we have to think things over and try to understand. A Communist Party member can't just have enthusiasm like fire, he also needs a head like ice . . ." Zhong Yicheng had reminded her to look reality in the face—but had she needed reminding? Odd, how a female comrade could be so pig-headed; Ling Xue looked at, thought about, and discussed problems with the feelings, viewpoint, and language of a Party member . . . but instructions had come down and Ling Xue had also been expelled from the Party register. A good comrade who had worked with children ever since her own childhood, who had participated in the revolution, who before had had no faults at all—just because she was loyal to their Bolshevik-salute love, had been given the death sentence by the government . . . Bolshevik salute, Bolshevik salute, Bolshevik salute! Suddenly tears welled up in his eyes.

1979

The gray shadow said: You're so pathetic! How come even then you couldn't see through things, how come you were elated like a fool when you went to reform through labor? You should see through things a little, don't believe everything . . .

But, my gray-colored friend, what right do you have to talk about seeing through things or not believing? You just hang back on the edge of life. Have you ever dived right into the water? Have you swum in the rushing current of life, floating and sinking? What right does someone who has never been in the water have to discuss water, attack water, deny water? You're so smart and cherish yourself so much, so you watch from the sidelines with cold eyes and shut off your own life, wasting it all away; so you get old and decrepit, your hair whitens and your teeth fall out, you mutter to yourself, letting out a sound that only a person with severe dysentery should make. Your life is nothing more than a misunderstanding, an anachronistic catastrophe, a sad sound, and that's all. Why can't you see through yourself? Do you have to live on?

1970

What did you say? You fervently love the Party? If you fervently love the Party why did the Party cancel your Party membership ticket? The logic of a genius! It presses on irresistibly, with the ease of a knife cutting through butter. What is a Party ticket, anyway?

Surely China doesn't give out Party tickets just like rice coupons, meat coupons, cotton coupons, and oil coupons? What can you exchange your Party ticket for? How much are they bought and sold for on the black market?

What did you say? You fervently love the Party? Then why did the Party make you into a stooge? You're reversing a verdict, retaliating to settle an old score.

It's odd, what good does it do the country to have one more enemy? Can it raise the quality of steel produced? Can it raise the rice production goal for peasants? Or rather, why do we want to use every way available to mold an enemy form?

Atoned for your crime? Which crime have you atoned for? You still haven't cleared up the last account when you add a new one; if you add up all the old and new accounts you're guilty of monstrous crimes—death is too good for you. Xiang Lin![15] How is it that a Communist Party member living in socialist new China, a young man bursting with vitality, absolutely sincere and good, could have a fate like yours? The Chinese race, so great and yet so tragic.

All right, let's put your problems aside for the time . . .

15. Xiang Lin is a poor woman victimized by feudal society in Lu Xun's story "Benediction" (*Zhufu*).

Put what aside? What is Zhong Yicheng? A hat? A coat? A bottle for soy sauce?

First drive them out, then digest them on the spot . . .

What were they? A piece of cornbread? A saucer of cupcakes? Or a plate of oatrolls for which one needed a good appetite? After digestion what did they become? Urine? Feces? A burped-out belch or a fart?

The result of purifying the class ranks: Zhong Yicheng, male, born in 1932 in P——. Family background: urban poor. Personal background: student . . . Zhong went from immature thinking to extreme reactionary thinking, holds unspeakable personal ambition, and in 1947, without going through the necessary procedures, sneaked into Party organizations controlled by Liu Shaoqi and his agents, who worked in their false Communist Party . . . He is an unreformed capitalist rightist element . . .

Year Unclear

A black night, as if glued together and dyed black with ink, sticky and gooey, quivering and flickering, not formed but not without form. Completely white-haired, his two round eyes opened like two dried-up well holes, Zhong Yicheng clasped a walking stick and walked in the midst of frozen glue. The wild whistling wind coming from the boundless sky rolled along the endless open country and faded away into the boundless sea. Was it lightning? The flashes of light that go before an earthquake? Will-o'-the-wisp or a shooting star? It occasionally lit up Zhong Yicheng's shriveled-up face—skin covering cheekbones, a face that had aged in one morning. He raised his walking stick and beat into nothingness, as if he were beating on an old poor plank that gave out a tap, tap, tap.

Zhong Yicheng, Zhong Yicheng, Zhong Yicheng.

The sound that came out of him was old and far away, anxious and hollow, like the echo when one talks into a dry, empty vat.

Zhong Yicheng, Zhong Yicheng, Zhong Yicheng.

The black night was swirling, wavering, undulating, fluttering. The violent wind was surging, calling, scattering, flying. The mast tilted in the huge waves, the snowcap tumbled from the mountain peak, the liquid in the earth spurted out of rocks, heads rolled this way and that on the streets . . .

Zhong Yicheng, Zhong Yicheng, what's wrong with you?

Zhong Yicheng, Zhong Yicheng, he died.

After the lightning came an absolute darkness.

Silence without sound. Darkness without light. Water without waves.

So small, like a hundred violins a hundred miles away playing a weak sound, like a hundred fireflies a hundred miles away lighting up with a green glow, like a hundred Ling Xues a hundred miles away waving at Zhong Yicheng . . .

Bolshevik salute, Bolshevik salute, Bolshevik salute . . . what advice do you have for me? He wanted to chase this Bolshevik salute, he wanted to chase this advice, he wanted to raise up his head, so hard to lift, he wanted to open these eyes and gaze into the distance . . .

Another flash of lightning and he saw Zhong Yicheng. Zhong Yicheng was at Ling Xue's side, wearing an armband and carrying a torch. No it wasn't a torch, it was a painful, burning heart.

September 1978

Zhong Yicheng's diary:

"This morning I wrote an appeal; in twenty-one years this is the first time I've told the Party so much of what was on my mind. It makes you feel so bad that every person has only one life. You can't prepare beforehand for all you have to go through; you hear the call to go to battle before you have any experience. If everything could start over again, we would have so much less foolishness . . . but then, looking back over twenty-odd years of bumpy times, I have no regrets and blame no one. Nor do I feel empty or feel it was an unspeakable and unthinkable nightmare. I deeply believe that each step was not taken in vain. My only hope is that I have learned the lesson I exchanged for this unimaginable pain, blood, and tears, and that the real truth will regain its original face and be recorded in history . . ."

VII

Work, work, work! Millions of years ago labor turned monkeys into humans. Millions of years later in China, physical labor was exercising its great strength to purify thinking and create a new soul. Zhong Yicheng deeply believed in this. His fervent love for his country's mountains, rivers, and people, his desire to give himself, his ardor to atone for his crimes, the vitality of his youth, and his violently expressed poetic emotions, which he unceasingly replenished from life and could not cut off no matter how bad the situation was—all poured into cumbersome, or one could say, rather primitive physical labor in this mountainous region. He carried a basket full of sheep turds up the mountain on his back to spread on the fields as fertilizer, but two minutes after he had started off, it was just like the last step in making bean curd when you press in with a slab of stone—the sweat poured out from all sides like the water out of bean curd. He bent his back seventy degrees, studying the ways of the old peasants as much as he could; his legs were spread apart and slightly bent to help preserve balance. His two hands were free. Sometimes he swung them to and fro and his arms relaxed so much he felt himself floating. Sometimes he would form his two hands into a circle—this was a stance from the martial art *qi*

100

gong. To climb a steep slope one must move one's breath to the navel. With each step he felt his legs had great energy, his back had great energy, his heels were firmly planted, his feet on hard earth, and he was giving all of his body's strength and enthusiasm, as well as the nitrogen, phosphorous, potassium, and organic elements in the fertilizers, all useful for agricultural crops, to nourish our Republic's fields.

He scooped feces out of latrines. The smell of the feces made him feel glorious and peaceful. One bucket after another, he mixed the liquid with earth, feeling from his heart that it was really and truly delightful. He mixed it evenly, let it ferment, and strained it finely; the earth turned black and oily and the clay loosened. Then he put it on the horse-drawn cart, took it to the earth and scattered it; the wind blew the residue of feces into his mouth. He felt carefree, because he had been brought up by Mother Earth for over twenty years and now for the first time he could give Mother Earth a present.

Springtime arrived. He turned over the deep earth, his eyes looking straight ahead and his ears hearing nothing else, all of his muscles and all of his soul's energy and concentration on three movements: holding the shovel upright with a straight back, stepping down on the shovel, and turning the earth; then once again holding the shovel upright with a straight back . . . He became a plowing machine. Other than these three movements, he knew nothing. He raced to the earth like a motor car, starting to function as soon as he arrived on the spot; he performed these movements as if he were participating in an international competition. When his legs had no strength left in them at all, he would jump up and let all of his weight down on the shovel, using the weight of his body coming down to push the shovel, cutting sharply into the earth in one jab . . . His head got dizzy, but this just made him go through the cycle of his three movements faster and more mechanically, without any perception of his body. Labor, in which he forgot himself, was both difficult and delightful. In a moment an hour passed, three hours passed, twelve hours passed, and he had turned over a huge plot of earth! All the black pieces of earth were moist and held the imprint of the shovel head. He wanted to count the pieces of shoveled earth, but there were too many, more than the hairs on his head . . . So people really could do vitally good things. These things would not be thoroughly denied or repudiated in one morning . . .

In the summer he cut wheat. His upper body totally bare, he bent over from the waist and let the sun shine on his back. The sickle was so exquisite and full of life, like a nimble finger; not only could it cut stalks of wheat, it could also bunch them together, pick them up, and move them. He learned how to use the sickle and also a few tricky movements—swish, swish, swish and out would fly a clod of earth, swish, swish, swish and another. Eyebrows were such delightful things; everyone had two eyebrows; it was such a good arrangement, but sweat still ran down and blurred his eyes. When he straightened his back, the fields that just a moment ago had been covered so densely with wheat that the winds couldn't get through were suddenly open and clear, and he could see peasants working to one side, and mountains and rivers. A gust of wind blew by and he was so cool, so proud . . .

In the fall he cut twigs for weaving baskets. A rope was tied around his waist and his hand held a sickle. For months he had not felt a sickle in his hand, and he felt the happiness of once again visiting an old neglected friend. He climbed to great and dangerous heights and walked in pathless places as if he were walking on a plain. In one year, he had come to love the mountains, he had become a mountain person. Just like a hunter, he looked in the distance and yes, he saw it, among clusters of rocks and weeds was a hemp tree new this year, just the right length, of even thickness, with no spots or knots, not too young or too old. It took his breath away; he was wild with joy. He took several strides forward and leapt on it, grasping it with his left hand and lightly swinging the sickle with his right. With one swishing sound, a high quality hemp tree was in his hands, bound up, and hung on the rope around his waist. Then he lifted his hand again and discovered another goal, and once again climbed after it, as nimble as a gazelle, as agile as a deer, his body strong and vigorous, his eyes alight. . . .

In addition to his regular work with the peasants and cadres who had been demoted to the countryside, he and some other "elements" actively gave themselves or were given as many extra responsibilities as the others' daily load over again. At three in the morning, when it seemed as if his body had just hit the pillow, he started the "morning struggle" of carrying manure to the terraced fields and bringing down walnuts, dates, sugar cane, and radishes. As you walked on the path under the sky, the stars looked like they were right next to you and could be grabbed with an outstretched hand. At noon, when his mouth was still chewing salted vegetables and cornbread, he started the "afternoon struggle." In the evening, after he drank two big bowls of gruel, it was time for the "evening struggle." If the night struggle lasted a long time, sometimes he would get confused and be unable to distinguish the night struggle from the morning struggle. Other than the positions of the constellations, he could scarcely perceive any difference. People are truly resourceful. When they call their overtime work some sort of "struggle," they can get up an extra layer of extraordinary revolutionary fervor right away, just as if they were fighting, were in war and opening fire on their enemies, the capitalist classes, and their own thinking. If one does not die, the other cannot live; who would dare to take it easy?

If you are going to do it, then do it—compete, criticize, and praise, as soon as you have a chance. They were put into categories based on their labor and their adherence to discipline: those who had reformed themselves rather well—group one; average—group two; slightly below—group three; and those who continued to oppose the Party and socialism and were prepared to meet their makers with hearts of granite—group four. This kind of criticism and comparison had compelling strength. So the peasants reflected: "The 'elements' put everything into their labor, as if they are furiously stamping out flames. Seeing them work makes us afraid—they run carrying heavy things up the mountain, and leap coming down. You can hear them panting half a mile away. But this is nothing. As soon as they have some spare time they have to think about their crimes and think about how this "flame-stamping" labor can help them go a step further in seeing their own evil natures more clearly, and go a step further in thanking the Party for saving them . . ."

Zhong Yicheng came from the urban poor and his family was not prosperous. As he had reached the crucial age in his growth and development—eleven to fourteen—his family had been just at the point where they didn't know where their next meal was coming from. He had a small, thin build, and his wrists and ankles were especially thin. During the frantic meeting and work after liberation, he had never had the recreation, exercise, and sufficient rest a young person should have. And after he came to the country his nutrition was lacking. The peasants could buy some snacks from the supply and marketing cooperative, but regulations did not allow the "elements" to buy any food at all. Still, some unknown, interior, mysterious strength supported Zhong Yicheng and did not let him collapse during this harsh, severe labor. Of the many cadres demoted to the country, most of them worked much less than he did; this one would go to the hospital or that one would ask for time off, and some of them would go back to the city and no trace of them would be seen for half a year. But he clenched his teeth and went bravely forward, experiencing a new pleasure and comfort in this harsh labor. He even felt that the previous years, when he had been involved in work that did not require physical strength, were all a vain boast, far removed from reality, years frittered away. But now his four limbs and torso, his body and soul had all been liberated. All restrictions and taboos—one shouldn't do hard labor right after eating, one should sleep eight hours a day, one shouldn't get into cool water right after sweating a lot—were completely discarded. One day when they were eating noodles—a rare improvement—little Zhong Yicheng ate six bowls in one meal. This kind of extraordinary, hard-working, sincere, and doggedly enthusiastic labor linked his feelings up with those of the peasants. A peasant said, "When he first came I was really afraid a gust of wind might blow him away. Who would have guessed he would just go barging straight on through." The peasants loved to urge him over and over again, "Save a little energy, don't put out until you drop dead. If you get injured it's for life!" And some peasants quietly invited him, "Don't pay any attention to their restrictions; come to my house for a glass or two. I'll boil you a couple eggs, look how thin you've gotten!" The peasants' enthusiasm made Zhong Yicheng feel warm all over, but he was a criminal: how could he avail himself of the old peasants' love and concern?

There was one peasant's child, nicknamed Lao Si, just thirteen, who treated Zhong Yicheng especially well. He would give Zhong Yicheng a scoop of red dates, then in a while call him over to look at a katydid he had caught, just as if Zhong Yicheng and he were companions of the same age. If his family had baked two potatoes he would bring one for Zhong Yicheng to eat while it was still hot. He also made a cotton pad for Zhong Yicheng's basket so it wouldn't rub him when he carried it on his back. Lao Si helped Zhong Yicheng in so many small ways that Zhong Yicheng was both moved and afraid. He said to Lao Si, "You're so young but you're always so concerned about me!" Lao Si said, "I think you people are really too miserable here." As he spoke, tears swirled around in his eyes. "No, I'm not miserable. I'm a criminal!" Zhong Yicheng hurriedly explained. "Haven't you already reformed? If your thinking wasn't good how could you work so hard like this?" "No, we haven't reformed very well . . ." Zhong Yicheng kept mumbling on, trying to explain but not really knowing what he was saying.

They were supposed to have four days off a month, but the "elements" didn't necessarily get one day in two months. When they did get time off, it was announced all of a sudden. After breakfast in the morning, just as they were wiping off their shovels, the person in charge would call the "elements" over: "Today you're off. Make sure you come back on time . . ." This kind of announcement right as they were about to leave was supposed to be good for reform. When the announcement came that they were to have a complete rest, Zhong Yicheng one-upped them, pleading: "I won't rest . . ."

Ling Xue had written many letters, none of them scolding him for not taking time off, but rather saying:

". . . Knowing you're healthy and working hard, I'm very happy. But why don't you write poetry? Why isn't there any poetry in your letters? Didn't you say mountain life was quite delightful? I believe it is quite delightful. I believe that no matter how hard it is (you won't say so, of course) it's still sweet. Didn't you say you often think of me? Then send me a poem about the mountains and your work. Or just write a poem for me. Don't forget, I am forever the first and most loyal reader of your poetry. Now I might be your only reader. Maybe in the future you'll have lots and lots of readers . . .

"Why don't you seek my advice? My advice is for you to—write poetry. Don't be despondent or sad, or afraid of starting from nothing; I believe in you . . ."

Ling Xue's letters brought Zhong Yicheng confidence and dignity. He triumphed, he savored everything, and occasionally he wrote a short or not so short poem and sent it to Ling Xue. In Ling Xue's reply he got more advice and new inspiration.

November 23, 1959

One year passed very quickly, and the initial participation in labor, along with the wild elation and self-satisfaction that came from self-purification, was past. Zhong Yicheng was already used to life and labor on the farm. He was very dark and thin, his spirit hale and hearty. He had learned a complete set of skills needed to live—plowing, driving carts, feeding and raising animals, weeding, watering, weaving wicker baskets, threshing, sunning, stacking, and winnowing. He also had learned the skills needed to pass the days on the farm: chopping wood, fishing with his hands, picking edible leaves, digging out wild garlic, pickling salty vegetables and cabbage, making noodles from two kinds of flour. . . . Although he had grown up in the city, although he was a bit anxious in his work, although he still wore a pair of glasses that he hated and wanted to smash, his gait and manner got closer and closer to that of the peasants. At the same time, that enthusiasm to work and reform gradually weakened with the passing of time; what came after he had keyed up his stamina too much was an occasional emptiness of the spirit. They had put everything into reform, but who took an interest in their reform? They actively wanted to give an account of their thinking but no one would listen. Other than supervising their work and making sure they did not fool around on the job or secretly go and buy walnut cake in the marketing collective when they got off, the leader of the cadres who had been sent down to the countryside asked them nothing. They had no way to ask, either; they didn't know what error in thinking it was that had demoted them to the rank of "elements." At any rate the word "rightist" was stamped on their faces, and their contradiction with the masses was a life or death opposition, so they were only allowed to live according to the rules. No reckless talk or activity was allowed. They were watched carefully, but only to see that they did not depart from the correct stance.

Sometimes Zhong Yicheng felt confused. The leaders of the movement, that is, the "three-person group," the "five-person group," and the "movement office," as well as the entire organization, all of the comrades, and even he himself had expended a tremendous amount of energy in frenzied activity to dig out his true self. With great difficulty they had managed to see through the superficial phenomena of his membership in the Party, his work as a revolutionary cadre, his participation from childhood in the revolution, and his loyalty to the Party, and dig out an analysis of his true essence. Comprehensively, tightly, step by step, repeatedly, profoundly, and systematically they had criticized him, until he was thoroughly refuted. With great difficulty he himself had written over ten self-criticisms, altogether adding up to over 300,000 words, more than he had written in eight years of work at the office. Finally he wrote a self-criticism that even Song Ming thought showed "a good attitude and the beginnings of change." In this self-criticism he analyzed every sentence, every action, every thought, and even every detail of his dreams from his birth on; it was as meticulous as if he were splitting one hair into seven strands. No wonder it took so much time and strength, and so many words. (As well as criticism of him that was imbued with a stern sense of justice, there had also been, in actuality, a lot of well-intentioned but sharp pleading and warning, many sincere and honest attempts to straighten him out, and detailed and convincing analysis.) Was it only so that he could be cast aside and ignored after things were done with? Could it have been just to give the mountains the strength of another laborer? They were separated into categories according to their labor and discipline, but these categories were only to supervise them and urge them on; no one concerned himself with their thinking. They had become criminals because of their thinking, but after they became criminals their thinking was like dogpee moss (a type of wild fungus)—it had run its course and perished. It could be likened to a play on its opening night; when it is about to start, bells are rung and drums beaten, real knives and guns, the glow of light in the scene, men, women, old and young, such a busy place. Then, when the prologue is over, suddenly everyone is gone, the setting is taken away and the lights turned off. What is this all about anyway? What is it for? Didn't they say something about reform? Didn't they say that the labeling was only the beginning? Why haven't they followed it up?

Things, however, were developing. It was just that this development was a bit different from what Zhong Yicheng had expected. He had originally thought, wasn't the purpose of expending so much energy in criticism to delineate right and wrong clearly, and wasn't it to give him a dose of strong medicine, turn him around, and once again return him to the Party's embrace and the ranks of the revolution? Criticism was severe because expectations were high, and they hated the fact that iron could not become steel. Didn't the Party always take this attitude toward its own sons and daughters? But one year passed, and he increasingly felt that prospects of returning to the Party's embrace were dim. Papers and documents formalized the statement that "rightist elements are the agents of imperialism and Chiang Kai-shek," and the category of "landlords, rich peasants, anti-Party elements, bad elements, and rightists." Zhong Yicheng and the others were told to go along with the village landlords and listen to the admonitions of the public security police . . .

It's always easy to analyze abstractly the kind of thinking to which one subscribes and one's own ideas or emotional state of mind, also, to analyze what train of thought and what deathly serious, frightening peril these thoughts, ideas, and states of mind may represent. No matter how difficult, how hard, how much it choked one up, in the end his thinking was still a fruit with no set form but with great plasticity. Although it had a large bulk and could not be swallowed, with pulling and dragging, pushing and shoving, the fruit would end up being pulled to the ground in pieces and swallowed. As it was being swallowed it was helped down by a slippery something—Zhong Yicheng's firm belief that the Party would never destroy him, would never destroy its own foolish child. But many days had passed and the situation became daily more odious; the government's actual treatment of him was something entirely different from his beliefs. This child, who since he was a young boy had harbored a life-and-death hatred toward Chiang Kai-shek and the Nationalist political forces, and who had carried out a desperate struggle against them—from which day on had he become the agent of Chiang Kai-shek and the imperialists? And how could imperialism and Chiang Kai-shek still be such a big thing on the Chinese mainland after liberation? How could the brave, strong Chinese Communist Party, that now had all reactionary cliques terrified to death, have been fooled into recruiting, inviting, or appointing so many big and small agents? If imperialism really did have so many agents, if it could covertly seize every opportunity like this, how could it have broken down so quickly and completely in 1949?

Forget it, if you think about it you can't figure it out anyway. The greatest advantage of labor is that it leaves you no time or energy for aimless thought. After working ten-odd hours, eating three meals of cornbread and half a bowl of salty vegetables, and drinking several bowls of water, who was in the mood to indulge in this kind of political deduction and idle metaphysical thinking? Shovels, sickles, cornbread, salted vegetables . . . his head was already filled with these things. Peasants were just like that, they really were different from intellectuals; they put all their strength into first supporting their lives. Their thinking ran around and around "How can I go on living?" and "How can I live a little better?" If they slacked off for a minute there was the danger of starvation. Even if intellectuals were in bad straits, they were still always above the standard line necessary to maintain existence, so they could reflect on some odd and

strange question: "What do we live for?" "How can I
live more significantly in the future?" The main reason
for this kind of worrisome self-reflection, therefore,
was too much to eat. To sum it up simply in one word:
"Stuffed."

When he thought about this he thought of nothing
else. His eyelids were already as heavy and dry as
lead, and his four limbs felt as if they had been
screwed on and could not move. "For—get—it": he
had just enough time to smile bitterly, but not enough
to take this bitter smile off his face before he fell
asleep.

Forget it, bitter smile, sweet and fragrant sleep
. . . for Zhong Yicheng, this was a totally new spiritual state, a new type of experience. Perhaps this held
a new direction, a turning point? Perhaps this was the
beginning of dejection and decline?

. . . a big wind, in the dark late autumn night a violent wind suddenly howled angrily, sand flew about
and frightened Zhong Yicheng awake. He got out of
bed confused, went to close the window, and saw a
light in front of him.

He stared in amazement. On the road a quarter of a
mile in front of his room, in the direction of the road-
construction engineers' kitchen, light from a fire and
smoke were shining in the wind. "Oh no!" Zhong Yicheng shouted. He knew that next to the kitchen was
the construction corp's storage room, and in it was
piled up not only lumber, but also a batch of newly

arrived dynamite and detonators. If the stove's fire
was not kept under control and the wind blew the fire
outside of the stove, if the cinders danced around in
the wind, in a matter of minutes the construction crew
would be surrounded by a sea of fire, and their lives
and property as well as the country's road repair materials would be swallowed up in flames. Furthermore, it would spread to the entire village, and with
such a big wind it was entirely possible that it would
spread to neighboring villages and the mountain for-
ests.

Zhong Yicheng shouted again, and not paying any
attention to whether the other "elements" in his dormitory were awake or not, dashed off in the direction
of the flames. The light from the fire grew larger and
larger; the kitchen had already caught fire from the
inside. "Fire! Fire! Fire!" Zhong Yicheng lost his
voice screaming, and woke up the soundly sleeping
workers of the road-construction crew. People yelled
and clamored, the ding-dong of bells rang out, and
some grabbed for their wash pans. The kitchen door
was still tightly closed and smoke was pouring out,
choking people. Zhong Yicheng was the first to rush
to the door; he grabbed a piece of wood as he went
and shattered the door with one blow. Fire and smoke
leapt out in one burst and Zhong Yicheng felt heat on
his face and body. He did not think about himself, but
went to beat, stamp, and roll about on the fire and
cinders . . . Soon afterward the crew brought pans of

water, baskets filled with dirt, and their one and only fire extinguisher. After a frenzied fight, the fire was quickly beaten.

As soon as the fire was thoroughly put out, Zhong Yicheng felt a piercing pain. Only then did he discover that over half of his hair had been burned off and his eyebrows were totally burned away. Burns were all over his face, his back, his hands, and his legs. He could not touch himself anywhere, in fact he could not even stand up because his feet were burned. His face twisted into an expression of pain, but before he could make a sound he lost consciousness.

Second Day

"Why did you go to the road-construction crew's building that evening?"

Because of severe burns, Zhong Yicheng had been sent to the commune's hospital. As he lay on the bed he saw the door to his room open, and the Assistant Chief of Cadres, a guard from the construction crew, and a special public security man come over to his bed. He felt boundless affection and warmth, and he forced himself to struggle up into a difficult sitting position. But when those three people came over to his bed, their faces were like steel, their muscles completely tensed, the light in their eyes hard, and their voices cold. When they opened their mouths what they said did not show concern for the injured one or gratitude to the one who had extinguished the fire. The questions they asked were in the style of an interrogation.

Zhong Yicheng answered the questions humbly and amiably. "I saw the light of the fire . . ." he said.

"What time did you see it?"

"I don't remember, but it was after midnight at least."

"After midnight and you still weren't asleep? What were you doing if you weren't asleep?"

". . . I was asleep, a big wind started blowing . . ."

"If a big wind started blowing how come just you and nobody else woke up?"

". . . . . ."

"Why didn't you ask your superiors if you should go to the construction crew's storage room? There's lots of dangerous materials in there, didn't you know that?"

". . . . . ."

"What were you after when you broke down the kitchen door?"

". . . . . ."

"Tell us carefully where you went, what you said, what you did, and who the witnesses are for the last twenty-four hours from six o'clock last night until now. Don't try to hide anything or get away . . ."

There was one question after another. At the beginning Zhong Yicheng showed his habitual cordiality, loyalty, and politeness toward comrades and leaders. Even though his body pained him everywhere, and he had not eaten even one day's worth of real food, and his stamina and mental strength could not take it, he still answered each question as correctly and carefully as he could. But the questions kept coming, each stranger and more perplexing than the last one. Also, the questions he had already clearly responded to would, after a while, come out of another person's mouth, from another angle and in a different form. All of his answers were taken down in detail, and then they racked their brains to dig out contradictions in them . . . Suddenly—so slow, so idiotic—he understood what was behind these questions: it was something unimaginable, something that could move the heavens and earth and make the Yellow River run upstream. His eyes turned black, his temples, nose, and neck oozed with the sweat of a sick person, his lips trembled, his nostrils flared, and his hands and feet turned cold, but he finally shouted out:

"Why are you asking these things? How can you be so suspicious? Chairman Mao, my old man, do you know . . ."

"Don't forget who you are!" Out of three separate mouths came the same warning. But Zhong Yicheng was already not listening to this warning. The earth and sky were swirling, his head was bursting, his body was sinking, and blood trickled out of his heart drop by drop. He knew he was going to die.

1979

The gray shadow: You deserve it!

Zhong Yicheng: Then, according to your intelligent opinion, if you saw a fire starting you wouldn't pay any attention? No matter that the workers, peasants, and property would all be destroyed by the fire? Humph!

August 1975

Five years had gone by since Zhong Yicheng had been sent to the village for "on the spot digestion." It wasn't just that going to the countryside, working, and eating a meal of flatbread steamed on the side of an iron caldron with the peasants was easy for Zhong Yicheng; it also gave him an important spiritual pillar during these years of confusion and disorder. Things from the past were all frozen solid. When people asked him about it, he laughed dully, "That's something from my past life." In twenty years of frustrations, his physical form, spiritual state, and manner all had changed. Harsh reality had opened his eyes; he still possessed the one fear that his body would be ground away, but he had totally lost the other—the spiritual feeling of having committed a crime. Also, while in the village studying agriculture and medicine, he had quietly written several poems. But no matter what his desire, no matter how much he struggled

against it, and especially in these last ten years of re-
peated criticism when certain people had cruelly recommended that he be "returned to the pot and cooked
again," he really had gotten old. Although in his inner
self he had preserved his self-dignity, when he came
into contact with people around him he had already
become used to unconsciously affecting an expression
of base humility. When he spoke, he was in the habit
of using tones of fear and trepidation. Life is stronger
than hope and time stronger than youth. What else
could he say?

But he still held on to one old habit of twenty years
ago: to be concerned about the important affairs of his
country. When he read the paper and listened to the
radio, he always forgot to eat. Looking through rumors and misleading lofty tones, he searched hard for
actual news about his country and the world; he was
burning with anxiety and unable to sleep at night . . .

Since the beginning of 1975, he had received one
letter after another from Wei's wife. In the letters she
said Wei had been implicated in some "February mutiny" case, and had only recently been released.[16] "He
caught an incurable illness; he often speaks of you and
wants to see you very much . . ."

Three times Zhong Yicheng asked for time off, and

16. The February Mutiny was a failed coup attempt supposedly
organized by army cadres in Beijing in February 1966. Authorities
now claim there was no such attempt.

finally got ten days of leave right after harvest—very difficult to get. So one afternoon in August he appeared in a small room only twenty meters square in the city of P——.

Wei's face was grayish-white. He had leukemia. These last two days it had acted up several times, so sometimes he was confused, other times clear-headed. When he saw Zhong Yicheng, his thin and withered face broke into an expression of relief. He said:

"So you got here after all. In this world there's been something that's always bothered me, and that's the '57 incident involving you . . ."

"It's over." Zhong Yicheng smiled in indifference and generosity.

"No, it can't go on wrong like this. I hope you'll write an appeal . . ."

"Am I so bored with life? I don't want to go looking for trouble," Zhong Yicheng said laughing.

"Stop it!" Wei was angry; he shut his eyes and did not speak for a long time.

"But how could that be possible? There was ironclad evidence and it's been almost twenty years. My self-criticism alone was 300,000 words . . ."

"Yes." Wei spoke in a small, weak voice. "At the time I opposed labeling you a rightist, but Song Ming brought out your own self-confession. A real idiot! But it doesn't matter that it's been twenty years or that your self-confession was 300,000 words long, or even that there are three million words in the verdict, as long as it's not fair, as long as it's not true. Even if it's as big as three huge mountains we can use the spirit of Yu Gong to dig them up.[17] The people have faith in us. But as for us, we used exaggerated animosity, extreme suspicion, and faithlessness to poison our lives, our country, and the hearts of those young people who loved and protected us . . . It's really a tragedy! Do you blame the Party, Zhong?"

Zhong Yicheng used to be full of great hopes on this question. Since that time many nights and days, many weeks, many months, and many years had passed. With the passing of each day he had buried his hopes a little deeper, finally so deep that he himself could not see them. In recent years he had constructed an even harder shell. To those who were on their way out of the countryside, he would nod in acknowledgment of his guilt, but to newcomers asking about things of the past he would show no interest at all in talking further, just like a mummy who came to life only with difficulty. He had already died once and did not want to die again, nor did he dare to reflect seriously even a little on what had happened in the fifties. He did not want to reopen a wound that was now covered with a thick scab as hard as steel. These feelings and attitudes fooled even him; sometimes he truly believed in

17. Yu Gong, "foolish old man," a character from a fable which was a favorite of Mao Zedong, succeeds through perseverance and will-power in moving a mountain from in front of his house.

his heart that he was no longer interested in or held opinions about this matter. This state of mind put him at ease and yet also terrified him. But today, at the bedside of his old superior who was soon to leave the human world, as he heard these forthright and faithful words which he had not heard for twenty years, he cried. He said:

"No. I blame only myself. If at the time my feet had been planted more firmly, if my self-criticism had been more factual, maybe things would not have come to this. And what's more, I'll tell you the truth, if places had been changed at the time and I had been responsible for criticizing Song Ming, I certainly wouldn't have been easy on him, and things wouldn't necessarily be much better than they are now . . . At that time, it was wherever they pointed, you attacked, whatever they said, you believed! As for you, I know several times you wanted to protect me . . . you wanted to reintroduce me into the Party, but couldn't . . . but now what can you say, in the end you couldn't even protect yourself . . ."

"People like me are a pathetic lot too." Wei spoke in starts and stops. "When you get right down to it, we were too fond of our careers. If right at the beginning of this problem with you people we had dared to speak out from a sense of justice, if we had been a little more awake and taken a little more responsibility, taken the facts instead of just the designs of those above us more seriously, if we hadn't been afraid to lose our jobs or be beaten, if we had stood straight and walked away, perhaps we could have conquered this domination by the 'left' early on. After it is announced that a person is an 'enemy,' it seems that we don't need to have sympathy or concern for him, or take any responsibility for him . . . Now, we've got what's been coming to us. It's been announced that we ourselves are capitalist roaders, reactionary gangs, and we've become landlords, rich peasants, anti-revolutionaries, bad elements and rightist agents, just as when you were called the agent of Chiang Kai-shek . . ."

"How can you talk like this, how could you have been responsible . . ."

Wei shook his head with difficulty, signaling Zhong Yicheng not to argue with him. "When I was in charge of regional committee work," he went on, "at the beginning, in the whole district we exposed and criticized only three people who had said rightist things. But later there was a directive that we should pull out 31.5 rightists from our district. Then the government put a lot of pressure on us and finally we couldn't control it, so we settled on ninety rightists altogether and implicated many more. Most of them weren't rightists. If we don't act now, I can't die in peace. I've already written a report for the Party . . . There will some time come a day when you can submit it, along with your appeal, to the Party . . . I have a responsibility. To have a serious Party, to be an earnest part of this Party, I have to take up my responsibilities in front of the people . . . But I'm proud too: look how the people supported us, even those comrades who were wronged looked with one mind toward the Party. In the past or the present, in China or abroad, what other party could move the people's hearts so fully and profoundly? This is a Party that has done a huge and far-reaching amount of things for the Chinese people. This kind of Party will naturally make mistakes, but we don't feel we have lived our lives in vain . . . Don't bear a grudge against our beloved Party . . ."

His voice got smaller and smaller, and finally his heart ceased beating. His wife knelt down, leaning against his body.

Zhong Yicheng took off his hat, showing his prematurely white hair. He stood in respect, silently bowing his head—

Bolshevik salute!

Zhong Yicheng had the report Wei had written concealed in his bosom, like a ball of hidden fire. Having this report made it even harder for him to live peacefully and drag on in his degraded life. He couldn't shut his eyes to wrong or remain at the mercy of fate anymore. But what else could he do? It would be difficult and fruitless to try and do something, but to force himself to do nothing, just endure, wait, and hope was even more painful. Time went by minute by minute, second by second, his hair and whiskers turned white one by one; after 1957 came 1958, from '57 to '58 were 365 days, then the 60's, and now it was 1975. Lots of

365 days had passed, and there were still years of 365 days left.

He showed Wei's report to Ling Xue without commenting on it, just saying, "We have to think of a way to hide it. No matter what, we can't let people know about it."

Later Ling Xue said in a high voice, "I've never admitted to what happened that year. In the end, who was the real Communist Party member? In the end, who committed a crime? History has to resolve it!"

"At least you were expelled on paper, at least for eighteen years you have not paid your Party dues."

"I don't believe it. Wasn't that part of our wages that was held back for Party dues? Aren't our tears, sweat, and youth all Party dues?"

What could he do? The stubbornness of a woman . . .

Ling Xue also said, "Since the principles of the conservation of energy and the conservation of matter work for the whole universe and the entire natural world, I often wonder what the great principle of conservation really means in terms of social and political life. Can facts, truth, and conscience really be covered up and extinguished? Can the peoples' desire, faith in justice, and loyalty be weakened and spent?"

"But this principle seems to come into play too slowly . . ." Zhong Yicheng waved his hands.

"After winter surely comes spring, and the sum of the inside angles of a triangle is 180 degrees. It won't be longer or shorter, more or less. I think that after a period of history when the balance of rumors, lofty words, blackmail, and slander is too weighted, things will tilt and start to turn over . . ."

"Of course I believe that too, so I wrote you more than one letter telling you if I died I could only have been killed, I would never commit suicide . . . and we have to live on the best we can, because there are still lots of people like Wei left in our Party."

November 27, 1959

But he didn't die, he lived. In his trance there was a warm hand that carefully nursed him, fed him, gave him water, turned him, helped him go to the toilet. But he couldn't see and couldn't speak. In his heart, however, he understood more and more.

Therefore, three days after the interrogators left, he slowly opened his eyes and saw, in a patch of black fog, a nurse wearing white clothes and a white hat. He thought he had seen the nurse's back somewhere before.

"Nurse!" he called lightly.

The nurse came over. As her face got closer to his, he called out in surprise, "Ling Xue!"

Ling Xue put her finger to her lips, motioning him not to speak. She told him District Secretary Wei had notified her to come and care for him. She told him

that Wei knew about the situation here and had come
to visit the previous day, but because he was still un-
conscious they had not disturbed him. Lots of peasants and construction workers were defending him
and had asked Wei that he be given honors and
awards. Wei told Ling Xue that after he returned to
the District Committee he was going to a meeting of
the Standing Committee and would bring up the issue
of removing Zhong Yicheng's label and getting him
started toward reinstatement in the Party.

Lao Si came, supporting his father and his old
mother, a poor peasant leaning on a walking stick.
Many road construction workers came too. They
brought eggs, fruit, peanuts, chestnuts, honey . . .
"We all know you're a good person," they said. This
was the greatest honor Zhong Yicheng got, and it was
from the people.

"But it's too hard to be a good person," he said.
"This matter of putting out the fire has opened my
eyes and made me see what a perilous position I'm
in . . ."

"But at the same time didn't it bring you hope?"
Ling Xue said. "There will eventually come a day
when our loyalty and sincerity will be recognized by
the Party. There may well be countless trials before
us, many attacks we haven't yet imagined may fall on
our heads, and the road leading to this day may well
be long and slow. But this day will come, eventually
there will be such a day!"

January 1979

That day finally arrived!

The months and years were ruthless, and behind them there were trials more ruthless then they. Zhong Yicheng's hair was white, and Ling Xue was no longer young. This couple received their exoneration and rehabilitation with total coldness, and in their eventual return to the ranks of the Party registry they were as unruffled as if they were observing the seasonal changes or the regularity of the sum of the inside angles of a triangle. Nonetheless, after they came out of the Party office in P——, they walked, hand in hand and with no prior agreement, to the bell and drum tower. From the top of this tower they had a bird's-eye view of the entire city; they could see the mountains, rivers, and fields on the outskirts of the city, and their eyes could follow along with the express train as it left the station and raced among the mountains and rivers straight to Beijing.

As if they had agreed to do so beforehand, they fixed their eyes on the rushing train. On the snow-covered ground the train looked like a fiery black dragon. Their hearts flew along with this train to Beijing. They stood for ages, watched for ages, but did not speak. But the words in their hearts were one and the same, they could hear the sound in their hearts. Crying hot tears, they said:

"Such a good country, such a good Party! The Yu

Gongs of our Party can still, shovel by shovel, dig up mountains and lies and treachery, and the Jing Weis of our Party can still, pebble by pebble, fill up oceans of foul and evil water.[18] Although the words 'Bolshevik salute' have gradually disappeared from our letters and speech, and people no longer use them and have forgotten that they include a word from a foreign language, allow us to use them one more time: Bolshevik salute, to Comrades Hua Guofeng, Ye Jianying and Deng Xiaoping! Salute to the comrades of the central governments! Salute to the true communists of the world!

"Twenty years of time have not passed in vain, twenty years of tuition were not paid for nothing. As once again, with justice on our side, we give the Bolshevik salute of struggle to the soldiers of the Party, we are no longer children, we have concealed much of our true feelings, we are experienced, we know suffering and hardship and even more the joy and value of victory over suffering and hardship. And our country, our people, our great, glorious, correct Party have had to hold many things back. They have gone through a lot, matured and become inestimably more intelligent. Only the bad have been frightened away by the thorns on the path of revolution. Only self-deceivers, deceivers of others, or those harboring evil

18. Jing Wei, a mythical bird that tries to fill up the sea with pebbles, is a symbol of determination.

intentions have shut their eyes to these thorns or even not allowed others to see them. No power will prevent us from following the brilliantly lit and inextinguishable road of reality back to its true nature or letting the bright road of constant faith go forward.

"Unite toward tomorrow; we must make true 'The Internationale'!"

Bolshevik Salute

The Chinese Intellectual
and Negative Self-Definition

While maintaining the moralistic stance of both traditional
Chinese literature and socialist realism under Mao, Wang
Meng's novel *Bolshevik Salute* utilizes modernist technique
and structure to undermine the positivistic and didactic ef-
fects of the realist message. Besides using the modernist
techniques of stream-of-consciousness, internal monologue,
unfinished sentences, jarring switches in scene, and emphasis on the psychology of the characters, the author also creates a modernist structural and thematic environment in his
portrayal of "reality" as perceived by the individual intellectual, and as circumscribed for the intellectual by the state.
There are three defining elements of this constructed "reality" which alienate the protagonist from his own personal
identity as an intellectual. They are (1) reality as a structural trap from which the individual has no hope of escape;
(2) reality as wordplay or as encompassed by a language
that does not correspond to "truth"; (3) the setting off of this
negatively defined "language reality" against the positive
but unavailable alternatives of physical labor or participation in the revolution. Through this modernist structure,
Wang Meng challenges the contemporary ideology which
states that an "intellectual" can also be "revolutionary";
rather, he claims that the terms "revolutionary" and "intellectual," as defined in China from 1949 to 1979, are incompatible and contradictory.

133

Structural Entrapment of the Individual

The experience of the protagonist, Zhong Yicheng, is detailed to the reader through a non-chronological series of twenty-six episodes, some lasting several pages, with the shortest only one sentence long. These twenty-six segments, which delineate Zhong's experience and perception, embody a dual structure that is a clear polarization of mental and physical events within the protagonist's life. The work maintains tight structural consistency, and the individual is portrayed as trapped in a mythically powerful—that is, inaccessible to perception or comprehension—dualistic structure from which he or she cannot escape.

The twenty-six segments of the novella can be characterized as positive or negative in a chart, which illustrates the structural coherency the author has established. In the chart, "CR" indicates an experience from the Cultural Revolution era of 1966–76:

1. Disorder	1957	−
2. CR, beating	1966	−
3. Party: love	1949	+
4. CR, beating	1966	−
5. CR, interrogation	1970	−
6. Party work	1949	+
7. Strong and fortunate	1957–79	+
8. Wei and Party education	1950	+
9. Anti-rightist	1957	−
10. CR, Song's suicide	1967	−
11. Gray shadow	1979	−
12. Party belief	1958	+ +
13. Generation of light	1951–58	+ +

14. Marriage, songs, wine	1958	+
15. To country	1958	+
16. Gray shadow	1979	−
17. CR, why?	1970	− −
18. Burning heart	none	− −
19. Diary; appeal	1978	+
20. Country—romantic	1958–59	+
21. Fire	1959	+
22. Interrogation	1959	−
23. Gray shadow	1979	−
24. CR, Wei's death	1975	−
25. Ling Xue after fire	1959	+
26. Retribution	1979	+

This chart shows an exact number of positive and negative episodes, with two extremely positive and two extremely negative events. The extremes are divided between the logical and the emotional aspects as explained below:

Positive-Logical

The high point of the positive-logical occurs in episode 12, when Zhong Yicheng's girlfriend and eventual wife, Ling Xue, lectures Zhong on a correct understanding of what has happened to him. The section begins with Zhong's declaration of faith in the party:

But I believe in the Party! Our great, glorious, true Party! The Party has wiped dry so many tears and opened up such a future! Without the Party, I would be only a struggling insect on the verge of death [p. 57].

The outcome of this long declaration is Zhong's decision that
the Party could not be wrong and he must indeed be a rightist. He decides to tell Ling Xue that they must separate,
and arranges a meeting with her to convince her of his
crimes. Zhong brings up several examples of his individualism, sentimentalism, and desire for glory, and finally breaks
into tears. Ling's response to this emotional outpouring is a
declaration of Zhong's innocence that is based on logical denial:

> No, no, don't talk like that, don't talk like that! . . . Don't
> exaggerate, don't be swayed by your emotions, don't
> make things bigger than they are, and don't believe
> everything you hear. The criticism of "Little Winter
> Wheat Tells Its Tale" was absurd! They're wrong to label
> you a rightist, they're mistaken. . . . Forgive me Zhong,
> in the past you didn't like to hear this, but it's true; you're
> too young, just too young. I mean you're too little, you're
> too innocent and enthusiastic, you love dreams too much
> and you love analysis too much. . . . Let's go together to
> try and understand those things we don't under-
> stand. . . . Maybe it's all just a misunderstanding, a tem-
> porary fury [p. 65].

Through Ling Xue's exposition, Zhong is able to regain
some faith in himself and in life.

Positive-Emotional

This positive-logical scene is followed by a positive-
emotional episode that is dated 1951–58, the era of the protagonist's greatest faith in the Communist party and in the
future of China. Using images of light and repeating the

word "love" several times in this section, Wang Meng recreates the enthusiasm of complete immersion in emotional identification with the nation, the Party, and socialist goals:

We are a generation of light; we have a love full of light. No one can take away the light in our hearts; no one can take away the love in our hearts. When we were young children, we struggled in the darkness. When we got a little older, we moved from darkness toward light. The night was too black, too dark, so we saw the morning as a flash of light, endless radiance. We shouted and leapt, running toward the light, embracing the light, not aware of the shadows there too. We thought the shadows had died with the black night; we thought the sun above our heads would forever be a morning sun [p. 68].

Negative-Logical

The negative-logical point occurs in section 17, when Zhong Yicheng is questioned by an unknown voice that appears to be his own mind. The questions focus on the lack of logic inherent in his faith in and love for the Party:

What did you say? You fervently love the Party? If you fervently love the Party why did the Party cancel your Party membership ticket? The logic of a genius! It presses on irresistibly, with the ease of a knife cutting through butter [p. 94].

Negative-Emotional

The negative-emotional point directly follows in section 18, with the date defined as "year unclear." In this section the images of light and love from the positive-emotional scene above are replaced by blackness, wild whistling winds, lightning, and a burning heart.

These four focal points of positive-logical, positive-emotional, negative-logical, and negative-emotional are the representative episodes of an entire structure that is organized around them. By characterizing each scene as positive or negative, Wang Meng portrays the individual as trapped in a preordered structure that throws him or her back and forth between two extremes of perception. By highlighting certain episodes as defined by logical aspects, and others as defined by emotional aspects, Wang formulates two ways of approaching the world that are impossible for the individual to reconcile in a personal identity. The sharp delineation between the positive and the negative in the different episodes establishes an absolutely dualistic structure, yet the even number of positive and negative scenes also implies a consistency; the individual's position fluctuates between the two extremes, and he is unable to perceive the larger structure that entraps him. Thus Zhong Yicheng is beset by doubts, yet only at the point where the negative and the logical coincide at their most forceful is he able to perceive the historical and national significance of his position; still, even at this time of ultimate awareness, his vision is only partial and is immediately counteracted by the negative-emotional scene which removes Zhong's ability to understand his predicament as a historical condition and places him back in the confining structure of individual emotional perception.

A possible reconciliation of the logical and the emotional approaches occurs in the final scene of the novella, the day of retribution in January 1979. The coldness with which the couple receives their exoneration, along with their linking of the event to "seasonal changes" and mathematical inevitability, implies that they have finally assumed a position of detachment that allows them to perceive both historical consistency and their own previous individual fallibility and entrapment:

> The months and years were ruthless, and behind them there were trials more ruthless than they. Zhong Yicheng's hair was white, and Ling Xue was no longer young. This couple received their exoneration and rehabilitation with total coldness, and in their eventual return to the ranks of the Party registry they were as unruffled as if they were observing the seasonal changes or the regularity of the sum of the inside angles of a triangle [p. 130].

However, following the pattern of the entire novella, with its switching from logical to emotional, and from positive to negative scenes, Zhong Yicheng and Ling Xue quickly return to an emotional identification with their past suffering and their new future:

> As if they had agreed to do so beforehand, they fixed their eyes on the rushing train. On the snow-covered ground the train looked like a fiery black dragon. Their hearts flew along with this train to Beijing. They stood for ages, watched for ages, but did not speak. But the words in their hearts were one and the same, they could hear the sound in their hearts. Crying hot tears, they said:
>   "Such a good country, such a good Party!" [p. 130].

As Wang clarifies, however, the implication of this emotional
identification with a past of hardship and a future of glory is
different from the entrapment of the past. The consistently
dualistic structure of the last thirty years will now be replaced by one in which the individual will not, as in the past,
function with a total lack of historical awareness, but will be
an intelligent, independent, objective observer of the present and of historical "reality":

> And our country, our people, our great, glorious, correct
> Party have had to hold many things back. They have gone
> through a lot, matured and become inestimably more in-
> telligent. Only the bad have been frightened away by the
> thorns on the path of revolution. Only self-deceivers, de-
> ceivers of others, or those harboring evil intentions have
> shut their eyes to these thorns or even not allowed others
> to see them. No power will prevent us from following the
> brilliantly lit and inextinguishable road of reality back to
> its true nature or letting the bright road of constant faith
> go forward [p. 131].

This portrayal, consistent with official policy in 1979 when
Bolshevik Salute was published, presents the past as an ab-
erration that political change has now rectified. This aspect
of the novel was seized upon by critics who supported Wang
Meng's modernist experiments; these critics claim the novel
illustrates the unchanging loyalty toward the Party and socialism that is characteristic of many of those who were per-
secuted in the 1950s, 1960s, and 1970s.[1] At the same time,

1. See, for example, Fang Xunjing, "Creating a New World of
Art" *(Chuangzao xin de yishu shijie), Wenyi bao,* August 1980: 33–

however, within this final episode the protagonist makes the same flip-flop switch between the negative and the positive, the logical and the emotional that has delineated his entrapment throughout the novella, thus implying at another level that the dualistic structure is still in effect, and undermining the optimistic presentation of a new consciousness, understanding, and direction. Although the entire scene of ultimate retribution is positive, as required by the positivistic tenets of socialist realism, it contains enough negative elements to allow Wang Meng to throw doubt on his superficial construction of a glorious future.

The protagonist's denial of the continuing potency of a previously mythical (that is, incomprehensible and unperceived) structure allows the novella to assume a didactic function characteristic of Chinese socialist realism. Through denial, the individual can reassume a moral position in society that was removed when he or she played the role of a cog unaware of the direction or overall movement of the greater wheel of society. The individual's renewed moral status comes not from moral awakening, however, but from the alteration of the direction of the "wheel," as society now insists on the significance and importance of intelligent individual input.

Therefore, Wang Meng gives the reader two contrasting visions. On the surface, the post-Mao reorganization of political and social reality has allowed the individual to escape structural entrapment and assume a morally valuable position. Within this restructuring, however, Wang Meng im-

---

37; and Li Tuo, "Realism and Stream of Consciousness" *(Xianshizhuyi he yishiliu), Shiyue,* April 1980: 239–44.

plies that the ups and downs of the past may still exist, and
that the individual will be caught in a new yet similarly pre-
defined structure and will be thrown back into a powerless,
illogical entrapment within the emotions.

Language and Negativity

In analyzing the referents through which the author characterizes Zhong Yicheng, we see that Wang Meng describes
the negative aspects of Zhong's life experience (1957 to his
post–Cultural Revolution rehabilitation) as formed by
language-related activities. Throughout *Bolshevik Salute*,
Wang maintains a strong scepticism toward language as an
indicator of "true" reality, presenting it rather as a self-
contradiction that is both the most significant and powerful
element of intellectual existence in post-Mao China, and at
the same time misleading and in some cases debilitating in
its ability to indicate reality.

In *Bolshevik Salute*, the ability of language to function as
a tool that can logically represent reality is undermined by
insistent emphasis on the perverting elements of language;
reality is an area of experience that must, by definition, lie
outside the bounds of inherent relationship to any form of
language representation. Consistent with this scepticism is
the book's dualistic structure, which breaks up into the
aligning parallels of the positive and the negative, and the
logical and the emotional. Language meets its greatest fail-
ure to interpret or represent reality when the positive and
the logical come together. However, in keeping with the

portrayal of the socially moral stance of the enlightened individual in a socialist country, the hiatus between language and reality is presented as a temporary state that will be rectified when the political environment is altered.

A closer look at the nature of the intellectual individual's plight reveals that his or her downfall is a result of reliance on language as a means of interpreting and representing reality. Furthermore, both society and the individual stipulate that language is the social phenomenon most significant in the definition of intellectual identity. Zhong Yicheng's trouble begins with the publication of a poem he has written about wheat:

> When wild chrysanthemums wilt,
> We start to come up;
> When frozen snow covers the ground,
> We are full of harvest's seeds [p. 4].

In Zhong's eyes the poem is the linguistic representation of physical reality; it is accompanied by a picture of the wheat-fields and chrysanthemums that strengthens this link. Wang Meng shows children as perceiving the unity between words and physical phenomena:

After reading his poem, a fat little boy dressed like a sailor asked his mother, "What is 'little wheat'? How much smaller is it than 'big wheat'?" "Sweetie, little doesn't really mean little, don't you see?" His curly-haired mother laughed, not knowing which words to choose. A girl with long braids read his four-line poem and wanted to go to the country to see the fields, the peasants and farmers, the cycle of the crops and the mill

where wheat turned into snow-white flour . . . What a
marvelous thing! [p. 5].

It is only much later in the novella, when Zhong is sent
down to the countryside for labor, that we discover that he
has never been to the countryside before; his "knowledge"
is not directly experienced, but indirectly gained, probably
through some language source. He suspects that his impres-
sions may have come from fiction:

> Clearly this was the first time he had come here in his
> life, not only to Goosewing Peak, but also the first time
> he had been to the mountains or the country. Why did this
> scene make him feel so unexpectedly close and familiar,
> as if they were kindred spirits? Could it be that he had
> seen a description like this in some novel? [p. 92].

Although for young children the poem creates an immediate
identification with the actual existence of wheat and flowers,
the poem is not the result of Zhong's immersion in and love
of the countryside that produced the wheat and flowers, but
rather a poetic fiction, the result of his immersion in and
love of poetry:

> Poor Zhong Yicheng had come to love poetry. (Some
> people say poets never come to a good end. Byron, Shel-
> ley, Pushkin, Mayakovsky—if they were not killed in a
> fight, they committed suicide, or they were locked up for
> having illicit affairs.) He read so much poetry, and, tears
> flowing, chanted it aloud; he stayed up all night, crying,
> laughing, mumbling, shouting. He wrote so many poems,
> going over and over them in a low voice [p. 4].

In the Chinese society of the late 1950s, Zhong's assumption that his poem is about wheat is equivalent to the naiveté of a child; as he comes to learn in the subsequent handling of his poem, for an adult language has no absolute referent but can be made to refer to any phenomenon, concept, or ideology.

The forced interpretation of the poem as political allegory is Zhong's downfall. The educated Chinese reader would undoubtedly perceive the double traditional-contemporary implication of an obvious linking of literary language to political events. Not only was political allegory a common form of writing in pre-modern and modern China, but also, because of the examination system and the literary education that supported it and prepared candidates for service as an official, mastery of the literary language and political power were closely intertwined. In the case of Zhong Yicheng, the interpretation of the poem seems to be ridiculously random; at the same time, the political nature of his opponents' analysis is only a common application of a traditional structural unity of politics and literature that is culturally designated and thus almost predetermined. Significantly, Wang Meng describes the nature of the analysis as something which "precluded discussion"; in other words, the logic of interpreting language as possessing political intent was internalized and natural to the degree that it required and allowed no explanation.

The criticism and labeling of Zhong underscores the importance of his use of language, both written and spoken. Zhong finds it odd that his "political history and actual performance" are not a concern of his critics; in fact, the critics do not even question him about it. When the Red Guards do mention his past membership in the underground Communist party, they focus on the language, both written and oral, that would validate this membership, which, of course, he cannot produce or prove:

"Your history is one of fabrication from top to bottom. You're not telling the truth. Your problem is very serious. People like you have more than enough qualifications for us to send you to the Public Security Special Division. Some not as bad as you have been executed. You yourself know for sure what sleazy bastards you all are. You entered the Party at fifteen and were an alternate member branch secretary at seventeen—who do you think you're kidding? Did you fill out a form? Who approved you? What oath did you take? Why was there only one person who recommended you . . . ?" [p. 24].

The criticism of Zhong's innate rightist orientation also focuses on his use of language:

Zhong Yicheng once ridiculed a certain leader for his verbosity . . . Zhong Yicheng once said this or that document, bulletin, or data was useless . . . Zhong Yicheng said there were problems in the relationship between the Party and the people . . . More and more, until Zhong Yicheng himself was totally confused [p. 12].

Zhong cannot analyze his emotions, but he is and for some time has been afraid of language; when he sees his colleague Song Ming "clutching a red pencil, engrossed in reading and making notes all over the critical essay" (about Zhong), he is apprehensive and remembers his fears at seeing notes on

Song's calendar in the past. The branding of rightists is carried out through the offices of critics who "exposed and criticized by means of slogans . . . the most inflammatory words possible." Even the faith in the Party which Zhong maintains throughout his trial is mediated through language sources rather than life experience:

> I knew the Party had been put together by an anxious country and a worried people, by the flower of the Chinese race and all the social classes; it was the sad, fervent song and the unselfish creation of a people willing to bear a cross for their liberation. Have you read "Wonderful China" by the war martyr Fang Zhimin? Have you read the poetry Xia Minghan wrote before he went to his execution? We have read them and know they are real [p. 57].

Bolshevik Salute places the manipulation of language at the experiential center for post-1949 intellectuals; the modernist structure of the story implies the difficulty of understanding or escaping from the predicament of an individual controlled by the language of any given historical moment. However, Wang Meng theorizes on the possibility of distance and perspective in the character of the Gray Shadow. The Shadow is uninvolved in the struggles of the time. In one image he dresses modishly, sporting long hair and a filter cigarette "dangling from the side of his mouth," and spends his time playing the Hawaiian guitar and listening to music from Hong Kong; in others he is a middle-aged or elderly man. The Gray Shadow has seen through and rejected the rhetoric of the post-1949 years and believes only in "love, youth, and freedom." Zhong Yicheng listens to the

Shadow and considers his standpoint, but ultimately he rejects his cynically realistic perspective as morally demeaning. The unattractive stance of the Gray Shadow implies the moral degradation inherent in an individual's being distanced from "reality," even if that reality is available only through an inaccurate and misleading language. Zhong Yicheng's rejection of the Gray Shadow is another example of the moralistic didacticism characteristic of post-1949 Chinese socialist realism.

A limited perspective is acquired by the character Ling Xue, who insists on viewing Zhong's situation as a "temporary fury" resulting from a deviation from the "normal workings" of the Party. Using logic to deny the validity of the "analysis" of Zhong's poetry, she criticizes Zhong for believing everything he hears and for his enthusiasm and naiveté. Like the Gray Shadow, she is criticizing Zhong for his lack of perspective on the manipulation of language characteristic of the times, in which values are inverted: "How can you say black is white and good people bad?" However, in that her social involvement is not as intense as Zhong's—she is criticized largely for her association with Zhong rather than for anything she herself has said or done, and she is not labeled as a rightist or beaten by Red Guards—Ling Xue cannot function as a moral alternative. Her role is limited to that of an intelligent if somewhat passive bystander who can only lend her support to the morally and socially engaged Zhong. The author's positioning of the logical, realistic character in a role auxiliary to the naive, enthusiastic main character devalues Ling's approach as somewhat too detached, although not to the point of moral bankruptcy characteristic of the Gray Shadow.

Although Wang Meng appears to blame the naiveté of people like Zhong for the excesses of the Cultural Revolution, the alternatives shown by Ling Xue or the Gray Shadow are not attractive or involved enough to function as criticisms of Zhong's emotional nature. Thus, although logical realism is (logically) at least temporarily correct, emotional participation turns out to be morally preferable.

Alternatives: Revolution and Labor

Contrasted with this language-controlled existence are two attractive alternatives: one is Zhong's earlier life as a worker for the revolution, and the second is the life of a peasant. Both revolutionary workers and peasants exist through their participation in concrete physical work as opposed to the largely bureaucratic existence that involves Zhong in paperwork (written language) and human relations (oral language). Wang hints at the possibility of an ideal world in which oral or written language possess a vital link to action and the material world as the offspring of human knowledge of that world. As previously noted, the poetry of Zhong Yicheng inspires children to want to visit the countryside and see the wheat, and when Zhong is sent to the countryside to begin his labor, Ling Xue encourages him to express the delight of country living in poetry. When he worked for the Party before 1949, the young Zhong used "progressive publications from Hong Kong and Shanghai, to inspire the minds of the young people and help them see the truth."

In all of these examples, the relationship between language and action or the phenomenal world is harmonious and without contradiction. However, in post-1949 society, this natural and beneficial link has been distorted, placing language and action in diametrically opposing positions, with action functioning as "true" reality and language as a misrepresentation of that reality.

Zhong attempts to bring up his past service as an active revolutionary in the Communist Party to defend himself against the "slander" of critics during the Anti-Rightist Campaign and of Red Guards during the Cultural Revolution, but, as previously noted, his actions are not as important as his words. His own description of his pre-1949 work shows not only the unification of language with action, but also the extremely physical nature of revolutionary work—something that has totally disappeared in post-1949 China. The description of Zhong and Ling's encounter with two remnant Nationalist soldiers is concrete in physical description and full of action:

Just as Ling Xue was about to respond to Zhong Yicheng's greeting, a volley of shots rang out. Two soldiers from the Nationalist Party's defeated ranks fled in panic along the dried-up riverbed. One of them had an obvious wound in his leg; the green bandage wrapped around it was stained red, and he limped. The other, a tall man with a beard covering his face, carried a rifle; he looked like a demon. Zhong Yicheng jumped off the six-foot-high bridge onto the tall man, and they both fell to the ground. When he caught a whiff of the pungent, moldy smell of the man's body, Zhong Yicheng raised his stick and called

out, "Put down your guns and put up your hands!" The
students all rushed over and encircled them [p. 20].

The speeches of the leaders as they describe the victories
and plans of the Party are perfect embodiments of their experience as active revolutionaries in the field, and Zhong
feels they have given him a "totally new way of thinking and
speaking," new concepts, and a "new language" that re-
places the "empty claptrap" and "officialese" of previous
years. Zhong characterizes their words as "forthright, logical, confident [and] surging with enthusiasm and strength."
     As the 1950s continue, this unification of word and action
disintegrates, to be replaced by a dualistic relationship that
is much worse than pre-revolutionary "empty claptrap" or
"officialese." True revolutionary *action* loses its position of
importance and does not even seem to be an option.
     By the late 1950s, the contrasting ideologies represented
by language and action are indicated in the "cure" for the
problems Zhong has manifested in his poem and words: labor in the country. Labor, the cure commonly prescribed for
intellectual ills since the thirties, is supposed to reeducate
his mind and thus reform his words. In actual Chinese society of the late 1950s, the promotion of peasant labor as an
alternative to intellectual work had been in effect for over
twenty years, yet in the novel it makes its first appearance
during the Anti-Rightist Campaign of 1957. Zhong's work in
the countryside turns out to be the opposite of his life as a
bureaucrat; replacing speeches, essays, and critiques is
hard physical labor. Zhong believes in the efficacy of the
cure:

> Millions of years ago labor turned monkeys into humans. Millions of years later in China, physical labor was exercising its great strength˚to purify thinking and create a new soul [p. 100].

The narrative details the physicality of labor, describing the sweat that pours off Zhong's body and the feel of the earth at his feet. The most physically sensuous experience is the most elevating:

> He scooped feces out of latrines. The smell of the feces made him feel glorious and peaceful. One bucket after another, he mixed the liquid with earth, feeling from his heart that it was really and truly delightful [p. 101].

Zhong "forgets himself" in labor, which is revolutionized and united with pre-liberation revolutionary fighting by the label "struggle":

> At three in the morning, when it seemed as if his body had just hit the pillow, he started the "morning struggle" of carrying manure to the terraced fields. . . . At noon, when his mouth was still chewing salted vegetables and cornbread, he started the "afternoon struggle." In the evening, after he drank two big bowls of gruel, it was time for the "evening struggle" . . . People are truly resourceful. When they call their overtime work some sort of "struggle," they can get up an extra layer of extraordinary revolutionary fervor right away, just as if they were fighting, were in war and opening fire on their enemies, the capitalist classes, and their own thinking [p. 104].

Zhong is confident that his life in the country has purified his thinking, but he is surprised to find that over time he loses his enthusiasm for reform and develops an "emptiness of the spirit." The problem is that Zhong and the other rightists sentenced to labor in the countryside are not given the opportunity to show that the cure has been successful; the "papers and documents" that label him a rightist are still more influential than his actual work. The primacy of language in determining identity, function, and role is still beyond Zhong's comprehension, yet in Wang's striking contrast between physical and bureaucratic work, language maintains its powerful position. Physical labor stands as a symbolic alternative, yet the dominance and prestige of language-related work is so great that physical labor remains only as a symbolic authority.

The absolute inability of language to transmit physical reality accurately is clear in the episode of the fire. Zhong risks his life to put out the fire, yet his action is distorted by the questions and comments of the interrogaters. Reaffirming his previously determined identity in their admonition ("Don't forget who you are!"), the interrogators illustrate the same random yet predetermined relationship between action (Zhong's action in the fire) and language (their interpretation). Their explanation of Zhong's action, which we as readers know is incorrect, is not merely a distortion of reality, but a reversal. Wang Meng locates this falsifying relationship between language and action as an absolute and overwhelming aspect of Chinese intellectual society from 1949 to 1979, the date of Zhong and Ling's exoneration.

In my reading of Wang Meng's novella as a comment on the intellectual's situation in contemporary China, I imply that Wang establishes the criteria through which the terms "intellectual" and "revolutionary" are incompatible. The only sure means to a "revolutionary" identity are unavailable to the intellectual; active physical participation in the revolution is no longer possible, and even if an intellectual engages in physical labor, his or her "true nature" as an intellectual is seen as always lurking close to the surface. Therefore, in *Bolshevik Salute*, modernist structure and technique work together to create an alienated, nonintegrated intellectual identity. Although Wang Meng's novella is carefully written to avoid criticism that may brand him as working against the Communist Party, he effectively challenges the insolvable dilemma that the Party has constructed for an individual attempting to define himself or herself as both "intellectual" and "revolutionary."